"Who knows when I might be in your bed again?

Kaden stopped to consider Pippa's words. Oh yeah, there were all sorts of buts and second thoughts. She didn't seem like a one-night-stand kind of girl but maybe he'd read her wrong. It was just sex after all. A way to forget.

He studied her expression, thought about what he knew of her. Pippa Duncan was a sweet woman who wanted to make the world a better place. She wanted to help people. And this was her way of helping him. Somehow, in spilling his guts about the day's revelations, he'd become one of her charity cases.

The more he thought about it, the more Kade understood what Pippa was trying to do. What would it hurt to accept what she was offering?

He gave in to the need.

His lips skimmed her jaw, seeking her mouth. Then he took their kiss deeper, yet kept it quiet and dreamy, hovering just on the edge of desire.

He eased back to look at her and asked, "Are you sure?"

* * *

Best Friend Bride is part of the
Red Dirt Royalty series:

These Oklahoma millionaires work
hard and play harder.

Dear Reader,

I'm often asked about my writing process. Let me unequivocally declare that I am NOT a plotter. I start with characters, a theme and a vague idea of how to get from the opening sentence to "The End." Then I turn the characters loose to see what happens. Kade and Pippa took me to a place I wasn't expecting.

As I was driving one day, the Kenny Chesney song "There Goes My Life" came on the radio. That's the first detour they tossed at me. I already knew what Kade's backstory entailed but his challenges changed when Pippa threw me a curveball. I began to explore the parallels in Kade's and Pippa's lives and the obstacles they had to face individually and as a couple. This book took me to a place I understood well.

Growing up, when my big brother teased me unmercifully, my stock reply was "Oh yeah? Well, Mom and Dad waited four years and picked me out. They were just stuck with you." Adoption is something near and dear to my heart—as I'm an adoptee with several adopted family members. While I grew up knowing I was adopted, not every adoptee is told. How emotional would it be to learn you weren't who you'd always thought you were? The characters in this book are about to find out.

Kade and Pippa learn that family is about love. Some of us are lucky enough to make our own. May you always have the warmth and love that family brings!

Happy reading,

Silver James

SILVER JAMES

CLAIMING THE COWGIRL'S BABY

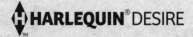

Recycling programs
for this product may
not exist in your area.

ISBN-13: 978-0-373-83859-2

Claiming the Cowgirl's Baby

Copyright © 2017 by Silver James

Printed in U.S.A.

Silver James likes walks on the wild side and coffee. Okay. She LOVES coffee. A cowgirl at heart, she's been an army officer's wife and mom, and worked in the legal field, fire service and law enforcement. Now retired from the real world, she lives in Oklahoma, spending her days writing with the assistance of two Newfoundlands, the cat who rules them all and the characters living in her imagination.

Books by Silver James

Harlequin Desire

Red Dirt Royalty

Cowgirls Don't Cry
The Cowgirl's Little Secret
The Boss and His Cowgirl
Convenient Cowgirl Bride
Redeemed by the Cowgirl
Claiming the Cowgirl's Baby

Visit her Author Profile page at Harlequin.com, or silverjames.com, for more titles.

To every person who has ever
created a family of the heart.

And with special thanks to my great
Harlequin team: Charles Greimsman,
Stacy Boyd, Tahra Seplowin, Keyren Gerlach,
Erin Crum and the magicians in the art department.
Y'all keep me on the straight and narrow.
looks shifty-eyed Mostly.

One

Kaden Waite was a simple man. Standing on the street staring up at the massive glass-and-steel tower that housed the offices of Barron Enterprises, he wondered why he'd been summoned here. Kade managed the Crown B Ranch for the Barron family. He belonged in the country, not here in downtown Oklahoma City.

Two women, chattering like blue jays, brushed past him, then slowed to glance back over their shoulders. Their appraisal embarrassed him.

Other people, men and women in suits moving at a hectic pace, pushed in and out of the building's entrance intent on their business. The city was full of rush and commotion. Kade liked to take his time. Especially today when he was out of his element. Bells from a church near the Oklahoma City National Memorial chimed, reminding him the hour for his appointment was rapidly approaching.

Removing his cowboy hat, he reached for the bandanna in his hip pocket, only to discover he didn't have one. Instead, his fingers encountered the crumpled envelope containing a certified letter requesting his presence today. And he had no freaking idea why. Cyrus Barron had hired him straight out of Oklahoma State University to run the Crown B Ranch, putting him in charge rather than one of Mr. Barron's five sons. Now that Mr. Barron was dead, was that about to change? Was that why Kade had been summoned?

He was dressed up—at least by his standards. Starched jeans with a knife-edged crease, buttoned-up shirt, polished boots. No bandanna to wipe the sweat from his forehead, no spurs jangling as he walked. Kade used an index finger to ease the pressure of his collar against his throat. Hat in hand, he entered the building.

Kade stayed pressed into a back corner of the elevator as it stopped on lower floors. People got on and off. A few women smiled. Several men did double takes before their expressions turned speculative. This wasn't the first time his presence caused that reaction. He wondered what people saw in him that created this response. Was it his Chickasaw heritage? His mother was a fullblood. He knew nothing about his father.

By the time the elevator doors opened on the thirtysixth floor, Kade was the sole occupant. He stepped into an impressive reception area defined by dark wood and leather. Both receptionists—one male, one female—

glanced up. The young man frowned, the slightly older woman smiled.

Hat still in his hands, Kade approached the desk. "Ah…good morning? I think I have an appoint—"

Smile still in place, the woman interrupted him. "Good morning, Mr. Waite. Heidi, Mr. Barron's assistant, will be here momentarily."

He eyed the plush leather couches and the tall-backed chairs in the waiting area wondering if he should sit down. The tall mahogany doors leading to the inner sanctum of Barron & Associates, the law firm headed up by Cyrus Barron's middle son, Chance, opened, making a decision unnecessary. A petite dark-haired woman bustled toward him.

"Good morning, Kaden." She extended her hand and he automatically shook it.

He remembered her. Chance's longtime legal assistant looked refined in her stylish business suit and low heels. Kade was careful not to squeeze her hand too tightly despite his nervous inclination to do so. Ever since Cyrus Barron's funeral, he'd fought down a sense of unease. Then a week ago, he'd gotten the certified letter.

Heidi ushered him down a long hallway. Her heels clicked on the hardwood floor only to be silenced when she stepped onto one of the expensive rugs lining the corridor. Stopping at a wide door, she knocked sharply and waited a count of five before opening it. Kade got the impression this was all stage dressing but he couldn't figure out why it would be necessary.

He made three strides into the room before the door

closed at his back with a quiet snick. Kade gazed at the people seated around the massive conference table, then glanced to the windows lining one wall. He could see for miles across the rolling countryside beyond the metropolitan environs of Oklahoma City. He refocused on the people in the room and didn't miss the looks they exchanged.

"Thanks for coming, Kaden. We'll get started as soon as Mr. Shepherd gets here." Chance's voice cut through the heavy silence.

Kade noticed the plates and coffee mugs on the table in front of the Barron brothers, and then located the long cherrywood credenza loaded with food and coffee decanters. Full of nervous energy, he took his time pouring a cup of dark roast coffee and choosing something to eat from the array of muffins, doughnuts and pastries.

Black coffee, a buttermilk spice muffin and the chair at the far end of the polished wood table. This worked. He had his back to the windows but faced the Barrons and the door. Except for the occasional sidelong look, the brothers ignored him—not that they paid much attention to each other either. He didn't want to think about his predicament. With the old man's death, he figured he was here to be fired, and if that was the case, he wished they'd just get on with it.

When Cyrus first hired him, Kade had been young and full of ideas. It wasn't until later, after years of watching the interactions of the Barron family from the outside, that he started wondering why the brothers didn't resent him. The ranch was their birthright. They'd grown up there and even though each had made his own mark in the world, the Crown B was still their home, still the heart of their family. To have its management turned over so completely to a stranger must have chapped their butts. It would have chapped his.

He'd poured his heart into the ranch for eight years. It was more than just a job; the Crown B had become his home too. And his passion. Their prime beef herds were the envy of cattlemen's associations in ten states and the horses he bred? They were coveted by horsemen the world over. His personal project had been to breed a "super stallion"—a stud to rival the American Quarter Horse Association's foundation studs. He now had a yearling colt that was the culmination of all his work.

If he had to leave the ranch, it would break his heart.

A sharp rap on the door jerked him out of his thoughts. When the door opened, an older man in a three-piece pin-striped suit marched in, set a briefcase on the conference table, looked around then fixed his unwavering gaze on Kade.

"Kaden Waite, I presume?"

Pippa Duncan pressed the pillow over her head. Jagged lightning danced behind her closed eyelids. The last thing she needed this morning was a massive migraine. She had too much to do plus a lunch date with Kade. No, not a date, she reminded herself. A lunch meeting. She needed to finish writing a grant and she had some notes she wanted to share with the Barrons' ranch manager to get his opinion.

She'd gone to high school with Chase and Cash Barron, had gone to parties and hayrides at the Crown B

Ranch. Her father and Cyrus Barron had shared the same country club, poker games and social set. Her mother had done everything possible to pair her off with one of the Barron brothers, and had never been particular about which one. She'd endured her mother's disappointed sighs at four weddings. Her parents hadn't been invited to the fifth so Pippa pretty much invited herself to Cash's wedding because she'd needed to get reacquainted with Kade. She needed his expertise and horse sense to build a string of horses for Camp Courage, her riding therapy program. That was her only reason. Okay, she'd crushed on the Barrons' ranch manager when they'd both been students at Oklahoma State, but she'd outgrown those feelings. Really she had.

It was all about business now because getting Camp Courage financed and running was her priority. Since Cash's wedding, she'd spent time with Kade at the ranch and he'd come to town for lunch or dinner a few times, all so she could pick his brain. Kade had volunteered with the Oklahoma State Outreach Riders, a group of students working with disabled kids and horses. When he called last night to ask her to meet him in Bricktown for lunch, she'd ignored the zing of excitement that coursed through her. Because…business. And she was too old for crushes. Even if there was a whole lot about Kade Waite for a woman to crush on. Beyond the obvious—tall, handsome, employed—he ticked off several items on her Perfect Man list. He was a cowboy— and that was the biggest priority. Yes, she was shallow like that.

If her head hadn't been pounding, Pippa would have

laughed. She was such a cliché—the rich debutante falling for a common cowboy. Except there was nothing common about Kade Waite. She'd known that from the first time she saw him at OSU when she was hanging out on the corral fence watching the rodeo team work. She wasn't too proud to admit fantasizing about the tall cowboy in the faded jeans with work-roughened hands, and some of those fantasies had gone straight to all things sexy. Because Kade starred in every erotic dream she'd ever had.

The prescription medication she'd taken for the migraine was finally having an effect and she could unsquint her eyes. She wasn't ready to remove the pillow yet, afraid her room would be too bright to bear. The migraines had begun to manifest more frequently, a worry that nagged at the back of her mind. She didn't have time to be incapacitated. She had grant proposals to write, stable and arena space to rent, horses to buy. Camp Courage was so close to becoming a reality.

Eyes scrunched closed, she lifted the edge of the pillow and peeked. When no blinding pain lanced through her head, she opened both eyes. The medications had fully kicked in. She still had tunnel vision but managed to focus on the clock next to the bed. She had time to make her lunch with Kade—if she hurried.

After showering and getting dressed, she was ready to head out when her mother met her at the front door. Pippa had been so close to escaping, but she knew she was stuck. She plastered a smile on her face. "What brings you out here, Mother?"

"I thought we might have lunch together, discuss your current activities."

"Sorry. I have a lunch date."

Her mother perked up. "Someone I know?" Then her eyes narrowed. "Why are you wearing those awful jeans and boots?"

"They're comfortable, and no, you probably don't know him. I'm meeting Kaden Waite, the Barrons' ranch manager. He's consulting on my foundation."

Millicent Duncan shook her index finger in Pippa's face. "I don't understand you at all. There are days I can't believe you are my daughter." Her mother closed her eyes in an obvious effort to control her temper. The bitter edge had smoothed from her voice when she continued. "I wanted to send you to ballet school. You wanted riding lessons. You have always had this obsession with horses. And helping unfortunate people."

Fighting her own temper, Pippa made her face blank. This was not a new argument. "It's my money, Mother."

"No. Technically, it was your grandmother Ruth's. Your father and I both tried to dissuade her from setting up that trust fund. We knew you would just fritter it away on—"

"Enough." She cut her mother off as lights started flickering in her peripheral vision again. Pippa needed to get away before the migraine precursors bloomed into crashing pain and roiling nausea. She squeezed her eyes shut and rubbed her temple in an unconscious motion.

"That man is not someone you should be seeing, Pippa." Millicent's voice grated on her nerves as the headache gained strength. "You need to stop all this nonsense."

"It's not nonsense, Mother. Now, if you will excuse me, I'm going to be late." Pippa slipped past her mother, shutting the door to the guesthouse behind her.

Pippa still managed to arrive a few minutes early. The patio of Cadie B's Southern Kitchen was one of her favorite spots—especially in late spring. Overlooking the Bricktown Canal, the restaurant catered to locals and tourists alike with a menu of southern cooking favorites. Her usual table hugged the outer railing but today, she opted for one closer to the brick warehouse building that housed the restaurant. The secluded table she chose was squarely in the shade and would remain so during lunch. She kept on her sunglasses just to be on the safe side. The perky waitress set a sweating glass of sweet tea in front of Pippa and she settled in to wait.

Thirty minutes later, she checked her watch, then her smartphone. Kade was officially late and he hadn't called or texted. Which was unusual. The guy really was a gentleman. She called him and when her call rolled to voice mail, she left a rushed message.

"Hey, Kaden. I'm at Cadie B's. Did I mess up and get the day or time wrong? Give me a call, please. Talk to you soon."

She wouldn't panic. But she reflected on her mother's pursed lips and condescension when Pippa mentioned she was meeting Kade. Even though she'd assured her mother this was a working lunch, Millicent Duncan seemed to have the idea that Pippa was dating him. Ha. She wished.

After no return call and repeated texts to Kade, three refills of tea and a waitress morphing from perky to pitying, Pippa lost her own easygoing demeanor. Her thumbs flew over the virtual keyboard on her phone as she typed an angry message.

CALLED YOU AND TEXTED. NO REPLY. IF STANDING ME UP IS YOUR WAY OF BLOWING ME OFF, YOU SUCK!

Kade's phone blew up with calls and texts starting about ten minutes after he walked out of Barron Tower. Numb, he'd climbed into his truck and started driving. Now he was northbound on I-35 headed home. Only it wasn't his home. Not any longer. A highway exit loomed and he jerked the steering wheel, taking the ramp at twice the posted speed. He didn't care.

Turning into the parking lot of a truck stop, he parked in the farthest corner. Stiff-armed, fingers bloodless as he gripped the steering wheel, he pressed back against the seat.

"Shut up!" he yelled at the cell phone. He wanted to turn it off. He wanted to slam it against the concrete and drive over it with his pickup. He wanted his life back. The damn phone pinged again. Another text. Wait…from Pippa?

Breathing like he'd just run a forty-yard dash, he opened her text. Standing her up? Blowing her off? He clicked over to voice mail. He had multiple missed calls from…what did he call them now? The Barrons. He'd refer to them as he always had. He couldn't wrap his head around what else they were at this point in time. Kade listened to Pippa's voice mail and winced. He'd blanked out about meeting her for lunch. Completely.

He hated texting. His thumbs were broad, unwieldy when it came to hitting the virtual letters but he didn't trust his voice. Thank goodness for autocorrect.

I totally messed up. Bad morning. I'm sorry. Really really sorry.

The big diesel engine of his truck rumbled as he stared out the windshield trying to marshal his emotions. Kade ignored the phone when it rang. It stopped after three rings. His text program dinged almost immediately, and he glanced at the message.

Will you please answer the phone so we can talk? What happened? I'd like to help if I can.

Pippa couldn't. How could anyone? He slammed his fists against the steering wheel. His mother had known. The whole damn time. She'd known who his father was. Had known the people he worked for were his half brothers. The sense of betrayal clawed at him, gnawed on his bones with teeth-jarring viciousness.

His phone rang again. He stared at the caller ID. Pippa. Accepting the call, he didn't say anything. Had nothing to say.

"Kade? Are you there?" When he didn't respond,

she continued. "What happened? I know you were supposed to meet with Chance this morning." Her voice trailed off but he remained silent. With a quick intake of breath, she gasped out, "Oh, no! Did he fire you? That's... They... That's despicable. After everything you've done at the ranch, after all the improvements, after...after..." She stopped and inhaled. "I'm so sorry, Kade. I can try to talk to them."

And she could talk to them. She was part of their social class. He knew she'd gone to school with the twins, Chase and Cash. Grew up knowing all of the brothers. His brothers. Half brothers, he amended. And wasn't that a kick in the ass. He closed his eyes, leaning back against the headrest.

Feeling exhausted, he huffed out a breath. He didn't need Pippa to fight his battles. He didn't need or want anyone involved in this very personal decision. He hadn't been fired, not outright. In fact, the Crown B could be his, lock, stock and barrel. "You don't understand, Pippa. It's not really like that. This is something—"

He stopped speaking. This really wasn't something he wanted to talk about. Not to her. Not to anyone. Not yet. It was too personal and he couldn't talk about it until he figured out what he was going to do. "Never mind, Pippa. Look, I'm sorry about lunch. You can't help, but thanks. Just leave it be. Please." So far, so good. He could finish this conversation without losing it. "I need to go. I'll...just...ah, later, Pippa. Bye."

Clicking off his phone, he leaned back against the headrest. He could get everything he'd ever wanted. All he had to do was accept the callous edict of a dead man.

Two

Pippa stared at her phone. Kade had very politely hung up on her without her getting another word in. What was going on? Before she could contemplate the situation, the waitress appeared again. If she didn't eat something, Pippa would pay for it later. She ordered then headed to the ladies' room. There was a line, and when she returned, her salad was waiting for her.

Still trying to decide what to do about Kade, Pippa ate and people-watched. That's when she recognized the five men occupying a nearby table. The last time she'd seen all five Barron brothers together had been at Cash's wedding. They were all incredibly successful. Clay was a US senator. Cord ran the family's oil company. Chance headed up a huge law firm. Chase normally lived in Las Vegas, Hollywood or Nashville as head of the family's entertainment empire. She seldom saw Cash, though he lived in Oklahoma City. He was president of the security company in charge of safeguarding all the rest of the family's enterprises.

"So what are we going to do?" Chance sounded glum and Pippa stilled. It was rude to eavesdrop but instinct had her skulking behind the arrangement of plants between her table and theirs to remain unnoticed.

"We can't make him accept." Clay shrugged and Pippa wished she could see his face. Who were they talking about?

"It's not like we hadn't figured it out," Chase added. "We've all hinted to Kade that we knew."

Wait…what? She was beyond confused now and waved away the waitress who was approaching with the iced water pitcher in her hand.

Cord glanced around the restaurant and Pippa ducked down as he spoke. "Leave it to the old man to screw up things all the way from the grave."

A waitress arrived to take their orders and no one spoke for a few minutes after her departure. It was Cash who reopened the conversation. "How did you expect him to react? Jump up and down for joy? The guy works for us. For the old man. Never once did Dad treat him as anything but an employee. Put yourselves in Kade's boots. He's told he's a bastard son and that the only way he can keep his job—keep everything he's worked for the last eight years—is to change his name. If he doesn't become a Barron, he's out on his butt." He met the gaze of each of his brothers and added in a sarcastic voice, "Yeah, I'd be thrilled to death with that ultimatum."

Pippa didn't want to hear anything else. Her first thought was to get to Kade. No wonder he'd stood her up. Maybe she was too softhearted, as her mother so often complained, but she wanted to find him, try to make things better. If she jumped up and dashed from the restaurant, the Barrons would see her. She had to wait. That meant dessert. And coffee. And more stalling.

She finally paid out and was just waiting for her chance to sneak away when a waitress and busboy began to clear the table between her and the Barrons. With a surreptitious glance toward their table, she slipped out of the chair and scuttled toward the door leading to the restaurant's interior. She now had one goal in mind—find Kade.

Walking to the parking garage, she considered what she'd overheard. Was Kade really a Barron? He'd never really talked about his family. Granted, she hadn't exactly been forthcoming about her own. She and Kade were friends but not particularly close. Not that she didn't want to know him better. She did because part of her remembered how she'd been that starry-eyed coed mooning over the handsome cowboy.

Cash said that Kade had to change his name or he was out. What exactly did that mean? Obviously, they wanted him to be a Barron, but did they mean to kick him off the ranch if he didn't? Her sense of justice surged again. Kade had told her she couldn't help, but she was determined to do something. Besides, what was the worst that could happen? He'd get mad, tell her to go away and that would be that. He'd still help out with the therapy program. Probably.

Before she could second-guess her motives, she headed toward the ranch, figuring that's where Kade would go. He'd lived there since graduating from OSU. She knew he was from somewhere down south—Sulphur or Davis or somewhere. Surely he wouldn't head that direction.

There was only one way to find out. She kept driving north. Her foot might have been a little heavy on the accelerator because she made the drive in record time. She followed the long, sweeping trip to the big house. No vehicles were parked there.

Pippa took a secondary road and headed toward the building that housed the ranch office. Kade's truck wasn't parked there either. She kept driving until she found the pickup in front of his house. She parked her Highlander next to his truck, worked up her courage and got out. After knocking on the door for several minutes and listening intently, she decided he must not be home. She stood on the porch and looked around. What would she do if she lived out here and was upset?

The open door of the main horse barn caught her attention. Had he gone riding? After picking Kade's brain about horse breeding and ranching, she understood enough about the Crown B operation to know that when the ranch hands rode horseback, they used the stock horses kept in the smaller barn. Kade worked and rode the blood stock stabled in the main building.

She headed to the barn and found Kade there. He stood in front of a stall, arms folded across the top of the stall door, chin resting on his fisted hands.

He looked…forlorn. Deflated. Utterly defeated. Pippa wanted to run to him, throw her arms around his waist and hug him until the stuffing came out, as her grandmother used to say. But her feet remained encased in emotional concrete.

"Go away, Pippa."

He hadn't looked up, but of course he'd know she was here. He always seemed attuned to his surroundings. There was no heat in his voice so she didn't move.

"Do you want to talk about…" She couldn't tell him she knew. He'd have to share that on his own. "About whatever has you upset?"

"No." He swiped his ball cap off his head and tunneled fingers through his thick, black hair but refused to look in her direction. "Just…leave me the hell alone."

"Don't curse at me. And I'm not leaving. You owe me lunch." She made a show of looking at her watch before glancing up at him, a smug expression firmly in place before she winked. "Though at this point, it is closer to suppertime."

Kade turned his head and her heart broke a little at the utter devastation etched on his face. His brown eyes were shadowed by a soul-deep pain. She moved then, walking toward him like she would a skittish horse. She stopped short of touching him, choosing instead to lean on the stall door in a mirror image of his posture when she'd arrived.

The yearling colt inside the stall whickered. Barron's Imperial Pride, Imp for short. "He's growing fast." Imp was Kade's crowning accomplishment and a safe topic.

"Yeah. Too bad I won't watch him grow up."

Or not. Pippa had to get Kade to tell her everything because this dancing around what she knew without tripping up was hard. She leaned a little closer to him, *accidentally* brushing her arm against his. "You can talk to me, Kade. Always. You know that, right?" He didn't say anything so she tried again. "We're friends, Kade. Friends help friends. I can see you're upset. Won't you tell me what happened today?"

He shook his head and the next words out of his mouth stabbed her heart.

"What makes you think we're friends?" Kade jammed the cap back on his head and glowered at her.

She flashed him what she hoped was a sweet smile before nudging his biceps with her shoulder. "I did drive all the way up here after you blew me off for lunch. Only a friend would do that." She considered her next words carefully. "Even if you don't want to tell me what's got you upset, I still think you need a friend right now, and I just happen to be here all handy and stuff."

She tilted her head to look up at him. "Besides, you're a growing boy," she said. "You need to eat. I'll even cook, provided you have something in the fridge."

Pippa wasn't going to leave him be, and part of him didn't want to be alone. "I'm not fit for company, Pippa."

"Yeah, and?" She grinned at him, totally unrepentant for intruding on his solitude.

Kade settled at her words and that surprised him. He didn't want company of any sort, but if he had to have some, Pippa would do. Seeing her at Cash's wedding, he'd remembered her from college, from when he'd catch her sitting on the fence mooning over him. He hadn't wanted a girlfriend then. He didn't want one now, especially not someone like Pippa. She should be with someone rich, like a Barron— He cut off that thought. Technically, he was a Barron, or could be.

He started to decline her offer but she was smiling all cute and sunny at him. Her long blond hair was caught up in a ponytail and the sprinkling of freckles across her nose went perfectly with her blue eyes. The quintessential girl next door.

It was just an early dinner. Between friends. And she was right. He needed to eat.

"C'mon, then." His voice was gruff as he ushered her out.

They exited the barn and Dusty, the ranch mutt, galloped toward them. He leaped up on Pippa and would have taken her to the ground had Kade not braced her with his body, one arm automatically going around her waist. He stiffened, fending off the dog with a terse command, then tensed more as Pippa pressed back against him. She shouldn't feel this good in his arms.

After releasing her, he kept his hands jammed in his pockets as they walked up the road to the house he'd called home since the day he'd arrived as the newly hired ranch manager. The place reminded him of the houses found on cattle and sheep stations in Australia. A wide porch wrapped around all four sides and the metal roof gleamed dully beneath the bright afternoon sun.

Pippa stumbled and he automatically caught her arm to steady her. "Pip? You okay?"

Her face had paled and she was squinting against the sun. Lips pressed together, she shook her head. "Migraine coming. Been fighting it all day."

He scooped her up into his arms without thinking. His mother suffered debilitating migraines and he knew what to do. "Keep your eyes closed until I can get you inside."

Lengthening his stride, Kade quickly got her into his dim living room. He set her on the couch and hunkered down on his heels. "What can I do to help?"

She reached blindly for him so he snagged her hand with his own. "I have meds in my purse. In the Highlander."

He pulled his hand away from hers reluctantly. "Keys?"

"Not locked."

"Be right back." Kade resisted the sudden urge to brush his knuckles over her cheek as he rose and headed outside. He returned moments later, her purse in hand. He didn't like the wince on her face as light spilled in from the open door.

"Sorry about not fixing dinner for you."

He brushed her apology away. "Not a problem. It's more important for you to lie down. I'm going to carry you into my bedroom, okay? It's darker in there."

She nodded so he lifted and cradled her. After she was settled, had taken her medication along with a long drink of water, she held his hand as he sat on the edge of the bed with her.

"I'll go away so you can rest."

"Don't. Please. I like the sound of your voice." A little smile teased the corners of her mouth and she patted the bed beside her. "And a girl likes to be fussed over. I'll be okay in a little while. I caught this migraine early." She offered him a tentative smile and a scrunched-up nose. "Besides, it feels a little weird being in your bedroom all by myself."

Concerned about her, Kade acquiesced. He stretched out beside her and moments later, she'd curled into him, her head on his chest. Was it wrong that lying here with her felt so right? Even so, he didn't want to talk about his situation, especially not to Pippa. He liked her more than he should, and liked her idea for a horse therapy program. He'd considered asking her out but figured she wouldn't be interested. Still, she was easy to be around. Too easy.

"Are you going to talk to me?" She asked the question without opening her eyes.

The feelings of bewilderment and resentment hadn't gone away. He didn't want to talk about his day and the choice that had been forced on him.

As a kid, he'd lain in bed next to his mom when her headaches put her down for the count. He'd read stories to her, and it always seemed to help. Since there was no reading material nearby, he began to talk.

Kade started out talking about the ranch, about Imp. He spoke of his grandparents and growing up on their small ranch outside of Davis, Oklahoma. He talked about OSU. About getting hired by Cyrus Barron. About making the Crown B his home. Without a conscious decision, he opened up to Pippa. He voiced his bewilderment at going from the only child of a single mother to having five brothers who'd grown up with their shared father, and expressed his concern over how they viewed him. Eventually, he got around to the feelings of betrayal engendered by his mother's deceit—a deceit he wasn't ready to confront her with yet.

He spoke until he was hoarse, hoping that Pippa had fallen asleep so she didn't hear the catch in his voice when he said, "Then the lawyer dropped Cyrus's ultimatum on the table. If I want to stay here, keep my home here, keep the Crown B..." He had to breathe before he could continue. "And it would mean keeping the ranch as CEO of the Barron Land and Cattle Company, it would mean owning Imp." And having more money than he could wrap his brain around.

Her hand pressed against his chest. "What do you have to do, Kade?"

"Turn my back on the only family I've ever known."

"I don't understand." Pippa's voice was soft as she craned her head to see his expression.

"To keep my place here on the ranch—to have absolute control over it, I have to change my name. I can't be a Waite. I have to be a Barron."

"Is that so bad?"

Kade almost shoved her away, remembered the pain she'd been in and forced his muscles to relax. Still, he needed distance so he eased out from under her and stood. What did she know about anything like this? Pippa was the beloved daughter of the Duncan family. They were rich, like the Barrons, while he'd worked for everything he had—all of which could be ripped away at the whim of the man who'd donated his sperm to create Kade.

He paced away from the bed then whirled to face her. "What would you say to someone who came to you and told you that you weren't a Duncan, could no longer be a Duncan? That you were someone totally different."

"But you wouldn't be somebody totally different. You'd still be Kaden. The name doesn't make a person. It's just a label."

He stalked to the edge of the bed and glowered at her. "Being a Waite shaped who I am, Pippa. My grandparents. My…" Anger surged again. He'd always been close to his mother. He'd adored her as a boy, respected her as a teen and admired her as a man. He'd never questioned their love for each other. Until that damn attorney read Cyrus Barron's will.

Pippa sat up on the edge of the bed, watching. After a moment, she spoke. "I'm going to repeat myself. The man you are is the man you've always been. Your family—the one that raised you—had a profound effect on who you are. You could change your name to John Doe, and you would still be the same man who is standing in this room. Understand?"

Her stomach picked that moment to grumble. "You need to eat," he said, relieved at the interruption. "Me, too. Do you feel up to food?" At her nod, he added, "I'll go see what's in the fridge."

"Okay," she replied. As he started to turn, Pippa slanted twinkling eyes at him. "But I need something else first."

He wrinkled his brow, not quite trusting her expression. "What?"

She crooked her finger, beckoning him, and when he stood before her, she crooked it again. As he leaned over, she laid her hands on his cheeks. Urging him to come closer still, she stretched up and pressed her lips to his. "You're good medicine. Thank you."

He enjoyed the kiss, brief though it was. Pippa was an attractive woman. Lying there in the darkened room with her, just talking, was intimate in unexpected—and not entirely undesirable—ways. "Okay. But I'm going to feed you now. Food is better medicine."

Kade slipped away from her. When she started to get up, he shook his head. "No. Stay put. I'll serve you dinner in bed." Which sounded far sexier than he'd intended.

In the kitchen, he made soup and sandwiches on autopilot while thinking about Pippa and what he knew about her. She was a sweet woman who wanted to make the world a better place. She needed to help people, and this was her way of helping him, he decided. Somehow, in spilling his guts, he'd become one of her charity cases. Just like he'd been for Cyrus Barron. His father. The word twisted in his gut. Bitterness welled up, but Kade reined it in. That wasn't fair to Pippa. She wasn't part of this mess. And while Cyrus might have been despicable, his sons had never really jerked Kade around. He needed to get a grip on his emotions.

The microwave dinged and he reached in to retrieve two bowls of homemade chicken noodle soup.

"Can I help?" He almost dropped the bowls at the sound of Pippa's voice.

Concentrating, Kade set the dishes on the counter without burning his hands or spilling the contents. He turned to gaze at her. She leaned against the door jamb, her eyes still looking a little bruised from the pain but

her lips—and he knew what they tasted like now—
curved up.

"No, I've got it." He glanced around. "I guess since
you're vertical now, we can eat at the table."

Pippa laughed, a deep, throaty purr that caused
Kade's brain, and other parts of his body, to go places
far beyond the gentle kiss they'd shared. "And forfeit
the opportunity to eat in bed? Not on your life!" She
whirled and was gone.

Gathering up bottled water, utensils and napkins,
Kade set up the tray and followed her. She was sitting
cross-legged on the bed, her back against the headboard.
He handed her the tray to steady, then settled opposite
her, doing his best to hide his body's reaction.

"This is nice," she said after finishing her soup. "Sitting here with you like this."

"Yeah."

"Want to know something?"

"Sure."

"I had a big crush on you in college."

"Uh-huh." Was she blushing? Kade swallowed hard,
feeling a little more Neanderthal than he was comfortable with. "I kinda figured that out." She didn't reply
and he fumbled for something else to say. "You were
cute, sitting on that fence mooning over me."

Tilting her head, she studied him, a half smile on her
lips and mischief twinkling in her eyes. "I had lots of
dirty thoughts about you while sitting there."

Kade opened his mouth but no words came out. Dirty
thoughts? His libido overrode his brain. "How dirty?"

Laughing now, Pippa shoved the tray away. "Really

dirty. Sexy dirty. Cowgirl-style dirty." She pressed her hand against her mouth. "I can't believe I'm telling you this. I blame the chicken soup."

"What's going on, Pippa?"

She glanced down at her hands clasped in her lap and her cheeks pinkened. "Probably nothing. I just…" She raised her chin and met his gaze directly. "I like you, Kade. A lot."

"The feeling's mutual."

"Is it?" She licked her lips and his eyes tracked her tongue.

Kade rolled off the bed, putting distance between them and easing the building pressure behind the buttons of his fly. What was Pippa saying? What did she want? For that matter, what did he want? "Are you done?"

"Yeah, I guess so."

Was that disappointment in her voice? Kade reached for the tray, hesitated, staring. "What's happening here, Pippa?"

Her eyes bored into his, as though she was searching for something. "I don't know." She breathed deeply. "A connection maybe."

Connection? Kade liked that idea probably more than he should.

"It felt good—my head on your shoulder. And the kiss. Maybe we could just lie here. Talk. Or kiss. If you want to."

If he wanted to? She was a beautiful woman. Sweet. And too good for him. But he definitely wanted to. Kade grabbed the tray, shifted it to the top of his dresser.

When he returned to stand beside the bed, he felt awkward. Pippa slid down until she was prone and patted the bed. He stretched out next to her and she rolled into him as if it was the most natural thing in the world. Maybe it was. Maybe he was overthinking things.

Yet, the more he thought about it, the more Kade understood what Pippa was trying to do, what she sought from him and sought to give back. She was kind and caring, and it dawned on him. She wanted to grant him tenderness, and if he gave in to the need for her, he would give her the same in return. This moment of... *belonging* was a gift. Aftershocks from the day's revelations continued to rock him, but Pippa could vanquish them. For a while at least.

His lips skimmed her jaw, seeking her mouth. Then he took their kiss deeper, yet kept it quiet and dreamy. And Pippa, this generous, concerned woman, opened for him. He held her as the kiss continued and they hovered just beyond the edge of desire. He discovered a sense of peace with her in his arms, mouth-to-mouth, body-to-body.

He eased back to look at her and asked, "Are you sure?"

She smiled, nodded and sat up. Neither broke eye contact as they unbuttoned each other's shirts. He felt her fingertips skim across his abs, his chest, and his breathing turned ragged. Working for control, finally steady again, he slid her shirt off her shoulders so he could touch her. His fingers glided over her surprisingly delicate skin. She was a cowgirl, with a cowgirl's strength. He was astounded when he discovered that fact, especially now as she sat on his bed, all but naked. A low hum thrummed in her, a sound of pleasure as she spread her hands over his chest while he skimmed his hands down her arms.

He gathered her close, eased her to the mattress and followed her down. They faced one another, touching, exploring, learning each other for the first time. He stripped the rest of her clothes off, kissing, licking, touching every part of her. He wasn't in a hurry when he kicked off his own boots and jeans, and he was male enough to enjoy the way Pippa's eyes widened and her mouth formed a perfect O at the sight of his naked body.

He wanted to spoil her so he offered lazy caresses that teased then soothed. His mouth found her breast, his hand cupping it for easy access. He wanted to tantalize, stoking her passion in a slow burn. Pippa arched and sighed beneath him, her fingers tangling in his hair. He swirled his tongue around her other breast, making her gasp.

Using his mouth and his hands, Kade ensured she had a long, slow climb to her peak. Her sighs tripped over into moans, and she quivered in anticipation, waiting, wanting, needing the pleasure. When he brought her to climax, she drew his head up, begged him with her eyes.

"Inside me." Her command rushed out on a hiss of breath. "Now."

Kade recognized her desire and slipped into her. She surrounded him, welcomed him with drenched heat, her inner muscles holding him in a fierce grip. They moved together, an intimate dance of retreat and advance so unconditional his heart pounded. She clenched around him.

"Kade."

When she spoke his name, the tenderness shattered him.

Three

Pippa considered the empty space beside her on the bed. The spot was cold so Kade had likely been gone for some time. She couldn't decide which was more awkward—waking up to the man she'd made love to for the first time, or waking up to his absence. Their relationship had changed—obviously—but for better or worse?

She listened but caught no sounds. Pushing off the covers, she rolled out of bed and stood, waiting to see if her head was going to cooperate this morning. For the first time in over a week, she had no vestiges of a headache lurking. Excellent. She grabbed her clothes and scuttled into the bathroom. She freshened up, using her finger for a toothbrush, dressed and headed toward the main part of the house. Which was empty. There

was no sign of Kade but for a pot of hot coffee and a
tented piece of paper propped up in front of it.

Opening cabinet doors until she found a mug, she
poured a cup, rummaged for milk and sugar, fixed her
coffee just the way she liked it and settled at the breakfast bar with Kade's note in front of her. Pippa swallowed a few sips while working up her nerve to read it.

"You're a big chicken," she chided herself out loud.
And she was. The fact that he hadn't stuck around
to face her the morning after—and they were in *his*
house—didn't bode well for their relationship to continue. If he was blowing her off, she'd have to figure out
a way to salvage things. She still needed his expertise
to get Camp Courage up and running.

Pippa stalled another couple of minutes while she
fixed a second cup. Finally unable to put off the inevitable any longer, she opened the note.

Morning, Pip. You were sleeping sound so I didn't
wake you. I have some work this morning and
need the early start. I left coffee. Hope it's not
too strong by the time you get up. Talk to you
soon. KW

Well, alrighty then. Pippa had no idea what to think.
It wasn't a Dear Jane letter. Not exactly. But it wasn't
a declaration of undying love, either. Not that she really expected such a thing. She just wanted a chance to
explore their relationship—especially after last night.
Her whole body heated just thinking about it. He was…
Her brain short-circuited and she puffed out a deeply

feminine sigh of appreciation. He had real muscles and his hands were work-roughened. And his…oh yeah, *his* was something to behold. And enjoy. She thought about splashing cold water in her face then glanced at the paper on the breakfast bar.

She reread the note. He'd called her Pip. Which is what her best friend called her. Plus, it sounded like what a guy might call his best friend's little sister. While Pippa might be an only child, her best friend, Carrie Longford, had two older brothers. Carrie had bemoaned the guy code loudly and often. Guys didn't date their friend's sisters. Nor did they date their sister's friend. Good thing Pippa had never been attracted to Carrie's brothers. But where did that leave her with Kade? She wasn't in the sister zone. Was his reticence due to her friendship with Chase and Cash? He'd also written that he'd talk to her soon. What did that mean? She obviously needed her BFF's advice.

She finished her coffee, rinsed out the mug and put it in the dishwasher. Her stomach rumbled from hunger. She also hadn't mentioned she was on birth control in the heat of the moment, nor had he brought up the subject. Wondering if she should wait until he came back so they could talk, she stared out the window. Movement at the ranch office building drew her attention. Uh-oh. A black SUV was disgorging tall, handsome men. Four of them. The only Barron missing was Clay.

Yikes! She had to get out of here. She could avoid driving by the office, though it involved a circuitous route. Kade's truck was still parked in front of the house and she figured the brothers would be headed here next.

She located her purse and keys, glanced around to make sure no other evidence of her presence remained and boogied outside. She twisted the lock on the door handle, hoping it would secure the door, and pulled it shut behind her.

Skulking to her car, she scrunched down behind the wheel, started the engine and eased away from Kade's house. Taking the back road toward the houses where other ranch hands lived, she eventually circled around toward the big house, gained the driveway and rocketed down it. Pippa didn't take a deep breath until she'd hit the section line road headed toward I-35. Then she started laughing. She was so ridiculous sometimes.

Kade sat on his horse. The small hill gave him a good view of the ranch buildings on the left and the grass range where a herd of Black Angus cattle grazed. He'd ridden out before dawn looking for some peace. He hadn't found it. He took off his Stetson and turned his face toward the sun. Wind teased his hair, loosening a few strands from the cord he used to tie it back.

He loved this land. Every scrap of it—the river to the south, the scrubby trees and rocky hills, the sweeping grasslands. He could admit to himself that he'd once wanted his own spread but after all the years here at the Crown B, this was home and he was satisfied. Until now.

Cyrus Barron. The man had been a master manipulator and he'd led Kade like a lamb to slaughter. Land management? *You're the expert, Kade.* Cattle breeding program for high-yield, Grade A beef on the hoof? *I trust you, Kade.* Want a "super horse" stud? *Do whatever you need, Kade.* And he'd fallen right into the old man's nasty web. Everything Kade worked for had been done to further the Barrons' brand. And he'd been proud of what he'd achieved.

Then the truth came out.

Shoving the hat back on his head, he judged the time by the height of the sun on the eastern horizon. Was Pippa awake yet? And man, wasn't that another can of worms he needed to sort out. He shoved that problem to the back of his mind. At the moment, he didn't have the time or energy to sort out his feelings for Pippa. But he worried last night had been a mistake. A big mistake.

Kade shifted in the saddle to ease the pressure in his jeans. Physically, last night had been amazing. Emotionally? He wasn't ready to go there. He liked Pippa. She was funny and cute and smart and sexy and sweet. Very sweet. She came from money—lots of it—and was the type of woman a Barron would date. Which brought him right back into that mental box he'd been trying to escape. He *was* a Barron. According to Cyrus's will. But he wasn't. He was Kaden Waite, half Chickasaw son of Rose Waite, grandson of William and Ramona Waite. He was a cattleman. He worked with his hands. He did *not* wear an expensive suit and tie.

But he'd put down roots in this place and it could all be his. His horse nickered and pawed the ground with a front foot. Kade loosened his grip on the reins. He'd freaked and stormed out of Barron Tower—and wasn't that one of his finest moments. *Not.* He shook his head, feeling rueful. His half brothers had risen to their feet, all of them talking to him at once as he'd lost his cool. Chance had blocked the door, tried to manage the situation. Kade scrubbed at his face as he remembered the scene. He'd threatened to coldcock Chance if he didn't get out of the way.

Chance held him in that conference room just long enough to say a few things—things he didn't want to hear. Take some time, Chance had said. Think things over. Kade heard the murmurs of agreement coming from the rest of the Barron brothers. Yeah, easy for them to say. They'd grown up as Barrons, knew who and what they were.

Since coming to work at the ranch, he'd walked a fine line between employee and friend with the five brothers. Looking back, he recalled the sideways glances and the hints. They'd suspected all along and he'd been… What? An idiot? Stupid? Clueless? Pretty much. He'd definitely been blind. He was still too angry to call his mother and too unsure to call his grandparents.

How could she not tell him? And why hadn't she gone after the sonavagun for child support? She'd worked hard all his life, sometimes two and three jobs until her paintings started to sell. His grandparents had all but raised him. All that time his *father*—Kade spit on the ground. Cyrus Barron had money. Lots of it. And he'd known of the bastard son living in Davis, Oklahoma.

The cell phone in his shirt pocket pinged. Jerking it out, he read the text from Selena Diaz, the ranch secretary. The Barron brothers had descended like locusts on the office. When was he coming back? He hated texting and she knew it. Stewing over whether to text back or call, and what to say, he chose to just ignore it.

He urged his horse off the hill and pointed him toward the far northwest side of the ranch. Selena's husband Pedro and several other hands were moving cattle today. They needed supervision, he decided. There was something soothing about pushing cattle, even with the dirt and grit. Kade was good at this job. It settled him. He was desperate for that right now.

Six hours later, Selena caught him in the barn as he unsaddled his horse. She was full of sass as she stomped toward him, face twisted into her version of a snarl— mostly crinkled nose, pursed lips and narrowed eyes. She stopped several feet from him, planted her fists on her hips.

"Did you lose your phone?"

Kade didn't look up. "No." He carried the saddle and pad he'd just stripped off into the tack room and returned with a curry brush.

She opened her mouth to start again, but Kade beat her to the punch. "Don't want to hear it, Leenie."

"Seriously? Then don't listen. Just stand there and don't pay any attention to me while I talk." When he continued brushing the horse, she launched into a speech. "Dude, you do not want to be jacking the brothers around. I know things have been really weird since Mr. Barron died. I mean the Crown B has always been sort of a…a sideline. Oh, sure, Cord was nominally in charge as president of Barron Land and Cattle but that was just a thing on a line of a corporate tax return because we all know he's into all that oil and gas stuff. You have no idea how excited Pop was when old Mr. B hired you."

Her father, Manuel Sanchez, was his ranch foreman now. Leenie and her sister, Rosalie, grew up on the Crown B. He tuned out her voice while he curried the horse. Then he turned his mount out in a big stall and set about watering and feeding the animal. Selena dogged him every step. He finally paid attention again when she grabbed his arm and jerked him around to face her.

"You could have at least replied to my text so I could tell them what was what so they'd get the heck out of my office. There was so dang much testosterone in the air even Dusty was hiding under my desk. What the heck is going on between you and them?"

Head lowered, he studied the tips of his boots. "Long story, Leenie."

She ducked and twisted so she could look into his face. "They didn't threaten to fire you or something, did they?"

How was he supposed to answer that? "Not your business."

Leenie straightened and glowered. "Seriously? I work for you, dude. If you get fired, it is most definitely my business. And FYI, they'd be stupid if they did. I grew up on this ranch. I know what it was before. And what you've done with it? Absolutely no comparison, boss man."

Kade removed his hat and scrubbed his fingers across the top of his head, loosening long strands of his hair. "It's not my work ethic being questioned."

"Then what the heck is going on?"

"Again, not your—"

"Business. Yeah, yeah. I call BS. I grew up with those five. Granted, I'm closer to the twins, but Cord and Chance spent a lot of time here too. You can talk to me, Kade. And if I can help, I will."

Shaking his head, he stepped around her, though he wasn't surprised when she pivoted and matched him stride for stride. He halted at the barn door, staring at the demarcation line in the dirt. Where he stood remained in shadow. One step and he'd be in sunlight. Was that a metaphor for something? He didn't have the energy to be philosophical and he was tired of the emotions bottled up so tightly inside that his whole body hurt.

"I'm Cyrus Barron's illegitimate son."

Four

Selena stared at him, her eyes almost as wide as her gaping mouth. "Holy cow. Talk about dropping a bombshell! Do the boys know?" She grimaced and rolled her eyes. "Of course they know. Hence the rugby scrum in the office today. Dang, boss. Talk about a tangled web. When did you find out?"

"Yesterday."

"Wow. Just…wow." She pushed his arm aside and moved close, her arms snaking around him. "Welcome to the family."

That startled him—both her action and her declaration. Leenie laughed and hugged him tighter as he tried to disengage. "I meant that in the figurative sense, not literally. Rosalie and I are sort of…" She smirked before finishing. "Kissing cousins." Laughing, she added,

"Big John caught us in the barn with the twins when we were kids."

She turned him loose and stepped into the late afternoon sunshine. "When you're ready to talk, I've got big ears and a closed mouth." She offered a jaunty wave as she headed back to the office. He started to follow her. He probably had work piled up on his desk but he didn't want to think about the ranch, the will, the Barrons or anything having to do with his predicament. He turned toward home. And stopped. That was the heart of the matter.

"It's just a house," he muttered, walking forward again. "Just a place where I sleep at night."

Not surprisingly, Pippa's Highlander was gone when he got there. That was a good thing, right? He didn't want to deal with her, with the inevitable questions she would ask for which he had no answers. He stomped up the stone steps and across the wide porch to his front door. Kade pushed through and stopped. The place was empty—as it was every time he returned. Why it bothered him now, he couldn't say. He hung his Stetson on the rack next to the door and headed to the kitchen. He'd missed lunch—his own fault. His stomach growled and he felt a little stupid for avoiding the Barrons. He still hadn't listened to their voice mails on his phone.

He grabbed a TV dinner and tossed it in the microwave, then popped the top on a long-neck beer. Retrieving his phone, he stared at the number of missed messages. He'd finished the beer by the time the oven dinged. He snagged another beer, peeled the plastic off his dinner and prepared to listen to what the Barrons had to say. He clicked on the speaker icon and opened voice mail.

"This is Chance. I wish you'd stayed to talk with us, Kade. I know this is a shock. Let's discuss things."

"Clay here. Welcome to the family, Kade. Talk to Chance."

"Dude, don't be stupid, says your big brother Cord. We're here when you're ready."

"Don't make me hunt you down." There was laughter and somebody said Cash's name. "Seriously, let's go get a beer, talk about this."

"Kade, this is Chase. Bad news, bud. You realize the wives are gonna be all over this. Fair warning. You know where to find me when you're ready."

Huh. Nothing at all like what he'd expected. He knew what the Crown B was worth. Millions. Why wouldn't they be upset at losing control of that kind of money? Wouldn't he, if he was in their shoes?

The messages from the Barrons continued in a round robin, before clicking over to the angry then conciliatory messages from Pippa. A stab of guilt burned in his chest and he glanced at the coffee maker. The note he'd left for her was gone. Yeah. He'd definitely taken the chicken way out of that deal. He didn't know why he'd kissed her…and more. He swallowed a gulp of beer. He was a guy and Pippa was gorgeous. He'd thought about getting her into bed—and the experience had been everything he could have hoped for. Well, almost everything. He still had a fantasy about her mouth that hadn't been fulfilled.

He didn't bother listening to the rest of the messages. He switched to the number pad and tapped in Pippa's phone number.

Pippa leaned her head back against the pool lounger and sipped her wine cooler through a straw. "Was I stupid?"

Her best friend occupied the next lounger, a frozen margarita in her hand. Carrie slurped from her glass. "Are you attracted to him?"

Tipping her sunglasses to the end of her nose, Pippa glowered over the top of them. "Is this where I say d'uh?"

"Then no. You weren't stupid. You saw what you wanted and you went for it. Rock on!" Carrie held up her empty hand, index and pinky fingers stabbing into the air while her thumb held down her two middle fingers.

"Seriously? You're flashing the Hook'em Horns sign at me?"

"That wasn't the University of Texas Longhorn salute—state college football rivalries aside." Carrie carefully set down her drink, sat up, extended her arms and waved both hands in the same gesture. "Rock and roll, babe! It's all about the rock and roll."

"Uh-huh." Pippa wasn't convinced but then again, Carrie had always been the wild child.

Carrie settled back on the lounger. "Look, Pip, you've always been uptight." She waggled her brows in mock apology. "You know I'm right. And Kade is hot. I mean *really* hot. Frankly, I'm confused about why he hasn't put the moves on you before now. I mean, seriously. Most guys get grabby on the first date. Not that you two have been on a real date. But, dudette, all those working lunches and dinners? Less work, more play." She rolled her eyes. "Leave it to you to find the last true gentleman in the state."

"There is nothing wrong with being with a gentleman." Pippa was slightly affronted.

"True that. I'm just saying they're few and far between. And I admit, I'm a little jealous. Look, did he have a good time?"

Pippa blushed to the roots of her hair. "I don't even know how to answer that."

"Well, he didn't kick you out after the big climax, right?"

"Carrie!"

"You two had some spectacular sex—at least I'm assuming it was because, girlfriend, I've seen that man in tight jeans."

Her face flaming, Pippa sucked down the rest of her cooler and pushed up out of the lounger. "I am not going to sit here while you embarrass the socks off me."

"You aren't wearing any. Just nod yes or no, okay? Was he good?"

Pippa chewed on her lips but jerked her chin to her chest in a brief nod. Carrie pumped her fist and uttered a breathless, "Yes!" before continuing. "And the man is a rancher. They're up before the chickens. I think it's sweet he let you sleep in. Frankly, I don't know many guys who would leave a girl in their bed the morning after their first time. Most dudes are too insecure or private or weird or something. Just doesn't happen."

"So…you think he'll call me? Ask me out on a real date? Or is this just one of those friends with benefits things?"

"Hmm…" Carrie pursed her lips and stroked her chin in an exaggerated gesture. "Yes."

Huffing out a breath, Pippa resisted the urge to throw up her hands in frustration. "Yes what? Yes, he'll—" Her phone rang.

Carrie let out a whoop at the ringtone. "Pip! Jason Aldean's 'Burnin' It Down'? That's gotta be Kade." She flicked imaginary tears from her eyes. "You make me so proud."

Scrambling, Pippa found her phone and winced at her breathless "Hello?" She made a face at Carrie while shushing her.

"Hey, Pippa. Uh…are you busy?" Kade's voice sounded uncertain.

She glowered at Carrie and made a shut-it motion with her hand. "No. Not busy. I'm just sitting out by the pool."

"Oh."

And didn't that word just drop into a void of uncertain meaning. Pippa suddenly felt the need to defend herself. Or make excuses. She wasn't sure which. She lived at home because her parents' Heritage Hills mansion was huge, and also had a separate guesthouse. While she had a trust fund that would pay her expenses, she was putting all her money, time and effort into setting up her riding therapy foundation.

"It's a nice evening so I thought I'd sit out here and enjoy the weather." Okay, that was totally inane.

"Are you wearing a bikini?" His voice had gone husky.

She glanced down her body and considered lying. "Um, no. Capris and a camisole."

"Oh."

And this time, there was a whole different tone and meaning to that syllable. A giggle bubbled out before she could stop it. "Okay. Guilty. Only it's not really a bikini. Just a two-piece."

"Mmm uh."

Pippa wasn't sure how to translate that and without thinking, she blurted, "Would you like to come over? We could swim. Maybe grill some burgers or something?"

Carrie gave her big eyes while covering her mouth with both hands as Pippa waited. Kade's answer finally came.

"Yeah. That'd be cool. Thanks. I'll be there in about an hour. Okay?"

Her heart was pounding so hard in her chest she was afraid Kade might be able to hear it. She nodded, realized she needed to speak. "That's great. Yes. Perfect."

"'Kay. See you then."

Dead air hummed between them and she panicked. "Oh, crud, Carrie! What am I going to do? I'm not prepared for a cookout."

"Breathe, babe. I got this. I'll run to Whole Foods, grab stuff. You go fix your hair and get out of that granny suit and into the hot bikini you bought for our trip to Aruba. The one with the sexy little wrap. And put on makeup."

"My parents."

Carrie was already at the door leading into the house. "What about them? They won't care." And then she was gone.

Would her parents care? She might live in close proximity but they most often went their own ways, very seldom crossing paths. Her mother always had some event or party and her dad was a workaholic. Pippa glanced at the Cartier watch on her wrist. She didn't have time to procrastinate.

Kade smoothed back his hair, feeling a little naked without a hat on his head. Despite being invited to a "pool party," he wore jeans and boots, and a crisp Western-style shirt over a clean white T-shirt. Pippa's parents had always seemed staid and traditional whenever he ran into them. While one of the Barrons might have gotten away with showing up in board shorts, he just wasn't comfortable. Again, he wondered what it would have been like growing up with the kind of money that guaranteed entrance and acceptance no matter where.

Not that he'd trade. Growing up on his grandfather's homestead outside of Davis had been perfect for a wild kid. He'd had horses to ride, ponds to swim in, trees to climb. He'd learned to hunt and fish and be a good steward of the land. Bill Waite had taught him to take responsibility, to work hard, to be an honorable man. Those lessons were priceless and there wasn't enough money in the world to get him to change. And that was the core of his dilemma.

The door opened, catching him off guard. Mrs. Duncan stared at him for a moment before saying in an icy voice, "May I help you?"

Offering a smile, he introduced himself. Again. "Evening, Mrs. Duncan. I'm Kaden Waite. Pippa invited me over."

"I see."

"Mom! Is that Kade?"

He heard pattering footsteps and then the door opened wider to reveal Pippa wearing… He blinked and tried to work up enough spit in his mouth to swallow. She wore a scrap of a bikini top with some sort of swirly see-through scarf thing tied around her waist. If it was meant to cover her up, it totally failed.

"Mom, you remember Kade." Pippa reached out and snagged his hand. "I invited him over for a swim and burgers on the grill."

"I see." The woman's tone hadn't warmed any.

"You and Daddy have that deal tonight at the art museum. You're gonna be late." Pippa was all bouncy and sweet as she maneuvered her mother out of the doorway so she could draw Kade into the house.

He wondered, briefly, if his reception would have been so chilly if he'd been introduced as Kaden Barron. The news hadn't hit the media yet, for which he was grateful and also curious. He wondered how the Barrons were keeping the story quiet.

He watched Mrs. Duncan leave. The woman didn't walk so much as glide and when she climbed the sweeping curve of stairs, he'd take bets that she could balance a book on her head, her posture was so stiff.

"C'mon out back." Pippa tugged his hand and glanced down at his clothing. "You did bring a swimsuit, right?"

He nodded, and indicated the small backpack slung over one shoulder. "I figured you had somewhere to change?"

"Of course! You can change at my place." She continued to hold his hand as she drew him through the house to a set of glass-paned doors leading to a terrace and pool. He caught glimpses of fancy furniture, antiques and artwork that probably cost as much as he made in a year. "What would you like to drink? I have that beer you like in the ice chest."

"That'd be great, thanks."

While the big house on the Crown B was expensively furnished with Pendleton rugs, leather furniture and Western art, it was comfortable—looking and feeling lived-in and homey. This house reminded him of a show home—each room decorated in a different style and looking pristine. No self-respecting speck of dust would dare land on any of the furniture.

Out on the patio near the pool, Pippa pointed him toward a second building—which had probably been either a carriage house or servants' quarters when the mansion was built at the turn of the last century. Two stories tall, it was made of the same yellow-and-buff bricks and stone with matching red tile roof.

"Technically, it's the guesthouse, but it's where I live." She offered a crooked grin. "Just so you know? You don't have to go to the front door. You can come straight back here and knock." She opened the door and he found himself standing in a combined living area and dining room. He glimpsed a full kitchen beyond the stairs. "You can change in here." She opened a door to a bathroom with a shower.

Quickly changing, he emerged and set his folded clothes on the couch. Pippa had disappeared but the outside door was open. He headed out and found her waving at him from the door to the main house.

"Beer's in the ice chest over there in the outdoor kitchen. I'll be back in just a sec. Mom needs something."

The outdoor kitchen was every bit as impressive as the one at the ranch, but for the life of him, he couldn't find an ice chest. Kade finally resorted to opening cabinet doors because he *really* needed a beer. After searching the entire kitchen, he discovered the built-in ice chest, with its own ice maker. This is how rich people lived—people like his half brothers. That's when he knew. Half his DNA might be Barron, but he'd never be one of them.

Five

Pippa knew her mother was watching from the windows in the kitchen—not that her mother spent much time *in* the kitchen. The woman's disapproval was almost palpable. She glanced at her watch, willing her mother to leave for the cocktail reception for some charity or another. Just her mother's cup of tea. There were times her parents' snobbery embarrassed her, and this was definitely one of them.

Yes, she'd insisted, when questioned by her mother a few minutes ago, the only relationship she had with Kade was of a business nature. And it had been—but for a few late-night fantasies with her battery-operated friend and a lot of what-if scenarios. Until last night. Pippa still didn't completely understand why she'd all but seduced him. She sipped her wine cooler and admitted that she wasn't sorry. Still, she needed to bring up the subject so she could let him know they were covered on the no-baby front. They hadn't discussed it. And she was a little bothered by that. True, she wasn't the most experienced, but it was a conversation she always insisted on—and not just because of pregnancy.

"You're thinking too hard."

She startled at Kade's voice. "Sorry."

"Nothing to apologize for, Pippa." His gaze shifted from her to the kitchen window. *Crud.* He knew they were being watched.

"I'm sorry. About my mother. She's…" How did she explain her mother's actions? "Well…she is who she is." His dry chuckle helped her relax. "She and Dad will be leaving soon." Hopefully. "Would you like to swim before we fire up the grill?"

Twilight was slow to fall this time of year but photosensitive lights were beginning to glow around the pool and landscaped garden. The air was also cooling and a light shimmer of steam rose above the heated pool.

"Or we could sit in the hot—" Car doors slamming cut off her words. At last! "—tub," she finished.

Kade waited until the sound of the car motor faded. "A swim sounds good. You don't have to get wet unless you want to."

She tilted her head, puzzled. "Why wouldn't I want to get wet?"

He waved a hand toward her hair. "A lot of girls don't like to get their hair messed up."

Pippa laughed and before he could react, she'd jumped out of her chair, ripped off her sarong and was sprinting for the edge of the pool. He was bigger and faster but she still hit the water in a sleek dive before he caught up. She was halfway to the far end when arms snaked around her waist and he halted her forward momentum. Kade turned her to face him and their legs tangled gently as they both treaded water to keep their heads above the surface.

"About last night—"

His lips pressed against hers, cutting off speech. One of his strong arms stayed around her waist while his other hand cupped the back of her head, angling her so he could deepen the kiss. This was good. Very, very good. Her arms circled his neck and she clung to him, mouth-to-mouth, their hearts beating almost in sync. The water lapped around them as his legs moved, treading to keep them afloat. Then he was standing, strong and sure, on the bottom of the pool.

She tasted the malty richness of the beer he'd been drinking. Warm steam rose from the water around them, kissing her skin. This was dreamy, she thought. Like a romantic scene in a movie. Pippa wanted to get lost in his kisses, in the feel of his hard body pressed against hers. They fit, and they shouldn't have. Still, they needed to discuss what had happened the previous night. That hard reality was a shadow on an otherwise shining moment.

Pippa shouldn't have been surprised to discover that she wanted him as much now as she had then. As the evidence that he felt the same pressed against her core, she knew she couldn't stall any longer.

"You're still thinking too hard," Kade murmured against her lips as he broke the kiss.

"Last night. I wanted to explain."

He loosened his hold on her as he reared his head back. "What about last night?" He sounded defensive and it distressed her that she'd been responsible for putting that tone in his voice.

"First, I'm on the pill. And as far as I know I don't have any STDs."

Kade's expression morphed into shock. "Wow. That was blunt. Okay. True. My turn to apologize. I didn't stop to think about a condom. That said, I'm clean."

She held back the sigh of relief. "Okay then. Now that that's out of the way, I—" She paused to breathe deeply. She only realized she was rolling her lips between her teeth when Kade's gaze dropped to her mouth and she felt his erection throb. It was all she could do to keep her hands on his shoulders because she wanted to fan her suddenly heated face. Luckily, with the falling darkness, she doubted he could see her blush.

"First." She laughed. "Or I guess second, I normally don't throw myself at guys."

His head tilted and his brows drew closer together as he watched her. "As gorgeous as you are, why would you have to?"

Okay, he could probably see her blush now, and she fought the smile forming because she was pretty sure if it got loose, she'd be beaming. "You think I'm gorgeous?"

"Absolutely."

"Oh." She was inordinately pleased. "That goes both ways, you know."

"Really? You think you're gorgeous?"

A laugh burst out and she covered her mouth. "No, silly. I think *you* are gorgeous."

"Ah," he said dryly. Still, Pippa could tell Kade was pleased with her admission.

"Ahem. Where were we?" She let her hands explore his shoulders, palms rubbing over warm skin and the muscles that came from tough work, not a gym.

"Right about here," he murmured, tightening his embrace and angling his head to kiss her again.

This kiss was slow, almost soothing, and obviously meant to distract her. He was working her into an easy arousal that felt natural and right. Her heart beat fast and steady and when he nudged the shoestring straps of her bikini top down her arms, she didn't care. When he held her, his mouth taking hers in a long kiss, she could forget where she was, forget her mother's snobbery, forget everything but the way he made her feel. Beautiful. Wanted. Being in his arms was beyond her ability to describe.

Pippa, in this moment, was his. She was all soft curves tucked against his hard planes. Pliant and eager as he kissed her again, she tasted sweeter than any woman he'd been with. He trailed kisses over the gentle slopes of her shoulders. He found the soft spot under her chin where her pulse beat and he pressed his lips there.

"Is this something special?"

He froze for a minute, her question taking him by surprise. Was it? He didn't want it to be. Or did he? He liked Pippa. Liked her smile, the sound of her laughter, the way she asked questions and chattered and the way she smelled. Did that make what they were doing special? Did it make her special? He owed her honesty so he said, "I don't know."

Kade swam them to the edge of the pool and braced her back against the smooth side. "This is new, Pippa. Whatever this is. I like you. I can say that and mean it. Do you think it's something special?"

Pippa pursed her lips as she studied him. He could almost see her mind working. "I don't know either. But it might be. Someday. Maybe." She blinked rapidly and looked like she wanted to take the words back before her expression showed resolve. "Does that freak you out?"

"Naw. Not really. I'm a guy. I don't like to play games. I want to know what you like. What you don't."

She wiped her forehead with the back of her hand and blew out an exaggerated "Whew! That's good to know."

Kade laughed. Doing so brought him in closer contact with her very feminine curves and he liked the way it felt. A lot. He was male enough that he just wanted to go with the here-and-now, but was that fair? He'd been in a bad head space last night. She'd been convenient. And willing. Was she more? And, being a guy, shouldn't he be a little freaked out by that thought? He didn't want to think. In fact, what he wanted was a repeat of last night.

"Will you trust me?" And wasn't that typically male too?

"I always trust you."

Her quick response stunned him. A warm glow

spread in his chest as a result. "I want to give you this. To give it to both of us."

At her nod, he clutched her waist and lifted. She unwrapped her legs so he could boost her to the edge of the pool. Spreading her knees, he moved between them. Kade tugged her bikini top all the way off and smiled. "I like the way you look, sitting here all wet and waiting." He flicked his tongue over her breasts, tasting and teasing each one.

She arched her back, her arms around his head, urging him to continue. He wanted her to float ever higher until he could send her flying. Desire rammed through him as she moaned softly, the sound and taste of her as rich as a sip of wine. He caught the sound of traffic in the distance, the slap of tires on pavement, but for all intents and purposes they were locked in a private hideaway. He caught a musical sound—a mockingbird. The thing evidently intended to serenade them.

Pippa chuckled; it was little more than a puff of air. "Persistent thing, isn't he?"

Kade captured her breast again and her moan drowned out the irritating bird calls.

The moon topped the trees around the yard and its light turned her skin luminescent. His hands found her hips, discovered the ties on the sides of her bikini and jerked. The material fell away. Now he could see all of her. Steam rose from the water. Kade was the least romantic man he knew, but Pippa was like some nymph in a book or movie.

"Beautiful," he murmured. Then he swept his tongue between her legs.

The act had her fingers digging into his shoulders. Her nails would leave marks but he didn't care.

"Ohhh," she sighed.

He teased her with his mouth but then he wanted to watch her so he switched to his hand. She was braced on her arms now, body arched, throat exposed, hair trailing over her shoulders. Pleasure was obvious in her expression and she seemed almost shocked. There was something endearingly innocent about her. The odd combination of Pippa's wide-eyed pleasure and wanton need turned him on like crazy.

His body throbbing, he pushed her higher, watched her eyes close as her breath caught in her chest right as her shuddering climax claimed her. Before she'd stopped, Kade had shed his swim trunks and had Pippa back in the water. He slid into her slick heat with a groan and found her mouth.

Bracing her against the side of the pool, he drove into her. Kade's body tingled, as if his nerves were raw-edged and exposed. Breaking the kiss, he closed his mouth over her breast, teeth nipping lightly. She cried out and dug her nails into his shoulders as her thighs tightened around his waist. Kade switched to the other breast, licking, playing with her until she was rocking, hard and frantic as she ground her hips against him.

Her body tensed, clamped down on him.

Kade lost his mind. His brain shut down, bombarded by sensations. Her body surrounded him. Their pounding hearts echoed each other. It was impossible to think around the intense pleasure. His body pulsed, plunging into Pippa over and over until he came, throbbing deep inside her.

"When I'm inside you…" His voice was rough and his vision foggy. "When I'm in you, I can't think. I can't…you kill me, Pippa." Words failed him so he lowered his mouth, crushed hers, his tongue sweeping in to claim her for his own. "Do you feel it?" he growled. "Do you feel what you do to me?"

She bucked against him, riding him hard, milking every last bit of his climax from him. She gripped his hair, dragged his mouth back to hers. "Kiss me."

He did. He devoured her mouth, nipping and sucking on her lips, her tongue until they were both breathless. Then he eased from her, slowly, so slowly his body shuddered and he had to hold himself rigid to keep both their heads above water.

"Whew," Pippa breathed once he broke the kiss. "Are we still alive?"

Kade laughed. She looked so smugly satisfied he couldn't help it. "I'm not sure." He didn't know how they could have survived. Even now, sensations pounded him, leaving his vision blurred around the edges and his ears ringing. "I'd ask if it was good for you—"

"Honey, that could almost make me start smoking," Pippa interrupted. "Because it feels like I need a cigarette. Or a drink."

This time, his kiss was playful and he was about to find her breasts again when the clearing of a throat froze them both.

"What do you think you're doing, Pippa? Have you no shame?"

Six

Pippa cringed and hid her head against Kade's shoulder. "She's going to go ballistic. I'm sooo sorry," she murmured against his skin.

Kade's arms tightened around her and he shifted his body so that he blocked her mother's view of her.

"Get out of that pool right now, Pippa Duncan." Her mother's demanding tone left no room for argument. "David! David, come out here. Come see what your daughter is doing."

Her father appeared at the back door. "Leave her be, Millie. Come inside and have a drink. Pippa is a big girl and if she wants to entertain a man—"

"Entertain?" Millicent tossed her hands into the air and stormed toward the rear of the house. "That's not what she was doing, David. They were… She… That man…" She was so incensed she couldn't speak in coherent sentences. As her mother marched up the stone steps to the door, Pippa's father handed her a crystal glass filled with amber liquid.

"Come inside, dear."

Her face flaming, Pippa watched the door close behind her parents. As soon as she was alone with Kade, she pushed away and struggled to hoist herself out of the pool. He gripped her hips in his warm hands and boosted her up. She scrambled to the nearest lounger, grabbed one of the large beach towels folded on the end and wrapped it around herself.

Kade joined her a moment later but she couldn't meet his eyes. "I'm sorry," she whispered. "You should probably leave now."

His thumb and fingers caught her chin. With gentle pressure, he lifted her head. "Look at me, Pip." When she kept her gaze lowered, he ducked down to her height. "Please?"

She sighed, complying with his request. "I'm sorry," she repeated.

"For what?" He looked amused but she got the feeling it wasn't due to her embarrassment.

"For…well…" She spread her arms. "For this."

While her arms were wide, Kade undid the tuck she'd made in the towel. Before she could react, he'd rewrapped it around her so she was completely covered and then he tied the two ends together for a more secure fastening. Finished, he winked, a grin creasing his face. "I think that's the first time I've ever been caught by a parent."

His wry smile was infectious and Pippa rolled her lips between her teeth to keep her own from matching it. "Seriously! I wanted to die." Then a giggle burbled out and she slapped her hand over her mouth to contain the sound.

"You still owe me dinner. I vote we order in pizza."

"Ooh. Good idea. I don't want to be within range of my parents just now." She leaned around his broad body and checked the windows overlooking the patio and pool. "But all the beer is in the ice chest."

"I'll grab what's left and meet you at the door to your place."

"And can you grab my stuff off the table?"

"You bet. Now scoot."

She scooted, and dashed upstairs just long enough to pull on a pair of shorts and a T-shirt. Then she rushed back to the door, hovering just in case her mother put in another appearance. Now that she was dressed— mostly—she could rush out to defend Kade from her mother's acerbic presence.

Pippa watched him move around the patio, a shadowy figure. But he wasn't skulking at all. He walked with purpose, like he had every right to be there as her guest. She smiled to herself. Since he'd dealt with Cyrus Barron, her mother—while not necessarily a pushover— probably wouldn't bother Kade at all. Straightening, she felt as though a weight had been lifted from her shoulders. Boys she'd previously been interested in had run for the hills whenever her mother got started.

As Kade approached, his hands and arms full of beer bottles and all her paraphernalia, she opened the glass storm door. Kade stopped in front of her and bent to give her a kiss before sliding on past. And that, she decided, was the difference between Kade and all the others. They'd been boys. He was most definitely a man.

"What kind of pizza do you like?" she asked, shutting and locking the door. She wouldn't put it past her mother to come charging into the house hoping to catch them in another compromising position.

"Anything with meat," he called over his shoulder as he headed toward the kitchen. She trailed after him. "Are you one of those veggie types?"

"Yes." She smirked as he rolled his eyes. "I like veggies with my meat, especially jalapenos."

That earned her an arched brow. "Well then, I think we can work something out. As long as those veggies are onions and peppers."

"Mushrooms and olives too. What kind of meat?"

"All of it."

She laughed at that. "Okay. I'll call it in." She did and surprised both Kade and the clerk on the other end of the phone when she read off the list of ingredients. "Yes, that's right," she said. "Onions, mushrooms, black olives, green peppers, jalapenos, and every kind of meat you have. Extra large, thick crust." She listened then glanced at Kade. "Do you want chicken, Canadian bacon and ham too?"

Laughing, he nodded. "Those are meat, so yeah."

She muttered something about clogged arteries, confirmed her address and that the driver needed to come to the rear house and hung up. She looked around, unsure what to do next.

* * *

After Pippa called in the order, Kade considered inviting her to share a shower. Two things stopped him—the tense lines around her eyes and the growling in his stomach. They only had a maximum of thirty minutes before the pizza arrived, and frankly, he wasn't ready for a case of "pizza interruptus."

Instead, he excused himself to grab a quick rinse off in the downstairs bath. After changing back into his jeans and shirt, he stepped out five minutes later. Pippa was nowhere to be seen. Then he heard water running upstairs.

Kade grabbed a fresh beer and settled on the couch. Surprised that the furniture was far more comfortable than it appeared, he found the TV remote and turned on the flat-screen hanging above the fireplace. Zipping through the channels, he found the Cardinals baseball game and sat back to watch.

Pippa was coming down the stairs when a knock sounded at the door. She sucked in a breath and tried to beat him there. He was closer, had longer legs and was faster. She slid to a stop at his side but she wasn't quick enough to keep him from opening the door. A bored teenage boy wearing a T-shirt advertising the local pizza place held a cardboard box. Pippa huffed out a breath. Kade glanced at her and wondered why she looked relieved.

"That'll be twenty-three sixty-four," the kid announced.

Passing the box to Pippa, Kade dug money out of his pocket and peeled off two twenties. He handed the cash to the delivery driver and said, "Keep the change."

"Thanks, man," the teen said with a little more enthusiasm as he spun around and jogged back to the beat-up compact car parked in the driveway.

Kade shut the door and Pippa called out. "Be sure to lock it."

She stood in the kitchen, her back turned to him so he took the opportunity to study her. Something was up. She was tense, uncomfortable. Maybe sticking around hadn't been such a good idea. He'd been serious when he said he didn't like to play games so he asked straight out, "Is something wrong, Pip?"

A plate clattered on the granite counter as she whirled to look at him. Guilt suffused her face. "No. Not at all. Why—"

"Don't pretend with me, Pip. What's going on?"

Pippa gave him her back and scooped the spilled piece of pizza back onto the plate. "Do you want Parmesan cheese? I have some fresh-grated in the fridge."

"Sure." He gave her time to duck into the stainless steel refrigerator before he pressed her again. "I'd appreciate an answer to my question, Pippa."

She braced both hands on the center island. "Nothing."

Everything about her—from the defensive hunch of her shoulders to the carefully blank expression on her face—screamed *leave me alone*.

"Really?" Sarcasm leaked into his tone and her eyes flicked up to meet his gaze.

"Fine," she huffed. "I'm worried that Dad won't be able to contain Mother. I keep waiting for her to march out here and confront us for our *lapse of decorum* in the pool. I've never quite seemed to live up to her expectations and tonight was just another glaring example of my lack."

"I don't find you lacking. Not in any way." Her startled gaze found his steady one. "You're smart, dedicated, responsible. And gorgeous. But I like you anyway." That startled a little giggle out of her. Good. He held out his hand and was gratified when she walked over to take it. He pulled her into a hug. "Families are weird. Trust me." And wasn't that the truth. Everything he'd discovered about his own turned his world upside down.

She giggled again and when her arms slipped around his waist, he felt her relax. "I've heard that. Mine are ultra-traditional, which is why I'm a disappointment. Mother expected me to make my debut, go to an Ivy League school, marry some scion of a rich and respectable family and become the perfect society wife."

"Oops," He said dryly.

That got an outright laugh from her.

"You can't live your life worrying about what she wants, Pip. You are your own woman. Live your life the way that lets you face yourself in the mirror every morning, knowing that you're the person you're meant to be."

She pushed back to look up at him. "Wow…that's rather profound."

Kade pasted a wry smile on his face. "You sound surprised. I can be a deep thinker when necessary."

"No, not surprised at all. Those things you said about me? Yeah, right back at'cha, buddy!"

He considered her challenge, remembering what

she'd said last night about his identity. She fought to be herself, not who her parents wanted her to be. Wasn't he trying to do the same? Except she would always have her name, her identity. He felt like he was losing his. And it hurt—enough that he didn't want to think about it anymore tonight.

He served up pizza and they retreated to the couch.

"Hope you don't mind me turning on the game."

Pippa favored him with a brilliant smile. "The only thing better than Saint Louis Cardinals baseball is Oklahoma State baseball. Well, and Cowboy football too."

"A woman after my own heart."

"It's important to be compatible sportswise."

Her dry tone got a laugh from him. "Truth!"

The rest of their evening was spent cheering on the Cards in friendly companionship. As the game was on the West Coast and went into extra innings, Pippa was asleep on Kade's shoulder when the Cards pulled it out in the thirteenth inning with a walk-off home run. Kade didn't want to enjoy having Pippa curled up next to him.

He'd asked her to trust him but he didn't trust himself. Not where this thing with Pippa was concerned. He was just selfish enough to drag her into his mess and she didn't belong there. She didn't belong with him. Not until he figured things out.

Then there was Mrs. Duncan. The woman had decided he wasn't worthy of her daughter, sentiments not too far from his own. Kade had no desire to put Pippa in a bad spot and he'd bet dollars to doughnuts that if his truck remained parked in front of the Duncans' house all night, her mother would give Pippa hell.

He needed to go, but should he leave Pippa napping on the couch or carry her upstairs to her bedroom. He glanced at the stairs. No problem getting her up there. Not joining her in bed? Yeah, that would be a problem. He needed to leave her right where she was or he wouldn't leave at all.

In slow motion, he slipped away and eased her down on a pillow. A soft throw was draped over the back of the couch and he took a moment to spread it over her. He gathered up his belongings and crept to the door. Kade paused halfway there, then returned to the couch. He bent over and kissed Pippa's forehead.

"I'll call," he whispered.

"Okay," she mumbled and snuggled deeper into the pillow.

Kade locked the door behind him and strode down the driveway. As he climbed into his truck, movement in an upstairs window of the mansion caught his attention. He paused, staring. A shadowed figure, too small to be a man, watched. Pippa's mother was something else. And that put him in mind of his own.

He drove away and pointed his truck toward the ranch. Once he was out of Oklahoma City, the only lights came from sporadic traffic and the occasional lighted billboard along the side of the interstate. Kade had about forty-five minutes to do nothing but think.

He should hash out things with his mom. She seemed as intent on avoiding him as he was her. After the reading of Cyrus's will, he'd left one angry voice mail for her. She hadn't returned his call nor had he made any further attempt to contact her. It felt weird, this gulf between them. Rose Waite had always been there for him—his biggest fan, staunchest champion and well… his mom.

But soon, he realized, he'd have to confront her.

Seven

Kade pulled into his mom's place a few minutes before noon. She didn't know he was coming. After a series of restless nights, partly due to some pretty lurid dreams involving Pippa but also the unresolved tension with his mom, he decided to confront her face-to-face rather than over the phone. Today, he'd done his morning chores on autopilot, then headed for Davis.

As he parked his truck, she appeared on the front porch, wiping her hands on a dish towel. She stood stiffly, waiting, probably guessing why he'd come. Hands jammed in his hip pockets, he stopped with one booted foot on the bottom step.

"Mom."

"Kaden." They stared at each other, neither of them moving. Rose was the one who broke the tension. "Well, come inside. I have iced tea made, and brownies. I can fix you lunch if you're hungry."

He climbed the four steps to reach her. On a normal day—before Cyrus died, before Kade discovered his lineage—he would have bounded onto the porch, swept his mom into a bear hug and swung her around until she was breathless and laughing. He didn't like this stiffness and distance between them. Resigned, he followed her wordlessly into his childhood home.

In her sunny kitchen, she pointed to the table set in the bay nook that overlooked the sweeping backyard. "Sit."

He did as she ordered and watched her putter around the kitchen filling tall plastic glasses with ice and pouring tea from a large glass jar. She'd made sun tea—leaving tea bags in the water-filled jar sitting under the hot sun. His mother drank iced tea year-round and only resorted to brewing it on the stove when the weather was too cold. She mixed a packet of sweetener in hers but handed his over plain.

"So," she said, settling heavily onto the chair across from him.

That was as much of an opening as she would give him. There was no sense beating around the bush. "You should have told me."

Rose crossed her arms over her chest and pursed her lips, studying him. He knew this look. He'd certainly been on the receiving end of it enough growing up. This time, he wasn't in trouble, though.

Kade pushed her. "I had a right."

"Did you?" She arched her brow and managed to look down her nose at him even though he was taller.

"Yeah, Mom, I did."

"Why didn't you ask me when you were growing up?"

"Why didn't you tell me?"

"It's not proper to answer a question by asking one."

"Sometimes, that's the only way I get an answer. What are you afraid of?"

That got him a bitter laugh. "You think I kept your parentage a secret because I was afraid? Of what?"

"Not what, who." He was watching her closely. Had he not been, he would have missed the tiny tick in the corner of her eye.

"I was never afraid of your father, Kaden."

"Then why keep it...keep *me* a secret?"

"You weren't a secret, son. Cyrus knew about you. There were...complications. If we'd met at a different time, or maybe in a different place." Her eyes turned dreamy as her gaze strayed to the scene outside the window. "I think he loved me in his own way. But he had demands on his time. He had to make a choice and it wasn't us." One shoulder lifted and fell in a negligent shrug. "It all turned out for the best."

Kade watched her as she had him earlier. "It almost sounds like you're defending him, Mom. Why? He left you. Left us."

"That's not exactly true, Kaden."

"Then tell me."

She pushed out of her chair and marched to the sink where she dumped out her glass of tea and fixed a fresh one. "Too sweet," she said without looking at him. "He paid my medical bills. Made sure I saw one of the best ob-gyns in Oklahoma City." She pivoted and braced her backside against the counter. She morphed her face into a scowl and mimicked Cyrus's voice. "'No child of mine will ever be born in an Indian clinic.'"

Rose almost smiled, her thoughts obviously far away. "He was all bluster, your father, but he did pay the medical bills. When you were born, he came to the hospital to see you. He…"

She turned away from Kade to stare out the window and he rose to go to her. She glanced up as he stopped beside her.

In a soft voice, Rose continued with her story. "He said you looked just like his other sons. Chance was just a toddler, the others slightly older. I think he was surprised, as if he'd been wondering if you were truly his, despite the blood tests and all. He refused to hold you. He just stood there looking. Then he offered to pay me a large sum of money to sign over your custody to him and walk away. I refused to accept anything else from him."

Kade tensed every muscle in his body to stay upright. "Why didn't you tell me this when he offered me the job at the Crown B?"

Rose continued staring out the window. "I thought about it. But…" She sighed heavily and faced him. She raised her hand as if to cup his cheek then dropped it to her side. "You have brothers, Kade. I wanted you to have the chance to meet them, get to know them. Maybe even be friends with them."

"Did you know about his will?"

She looked perplexed so he told her, his explanation spilling out in angry tones.

Her bewilderment morphed into regret. "I had no idea your father would do this. That he would saddle you with this decision, but I can't say I'm surprised."

She walked into the living room and went to the mantel above the native stone fireplace. He followed her. That fireplace held a lot of memories—hanging his Christmas stocking, being curled up in a sleeping bag "camping out" in front of it in the wintertime. Roasting marshmallows for s'mores. The heavy wooden mantel held a variety of knickknacks. Photos. A couple of trophies from high school sports. A belt buckle he won at the College Finals Rodeo. His mom took down a picture, one of him when he was about twelve.

"Were you ever going to tell me?" He tucked his chin and rubbed at the tense muscles on the back of his neck. "If he hadn't named me in the will, would you have ever told me?"

That question seemed to stump her, or maybe she just chose to ignore him. She walked back into the kitchen, with Kade trailing along, and she placed the photo facedown on the counter. Digging in a drawer, she came up with a screwdriver and started taking the back of the picture frame off.

"Mom?"

She stared through the window over the sink again. He moved up beside her to check what was out there, saw what she was looking at—a doe and her half-grown fawn nibbling grass near the tree line and an image much closer—his reflection standing next to hers in the window glass.

Families. As Pippa had said, they were complicated.

Rose handed him the piece of paper she'd retrieved from inside the frame. He took it, wordlessly, and unfolded it. It was an old newspaper clipping with a picture of Clay, Cord and Chance standing with their father at the opening of some building. His mother had cut this out of the Oklahoma City paper. He glanced at the photo of himself, lying faceup on the counter. For the first time, he recognized the family resemblance and wondered why he hadn't before.

His mother leaned against his arm and he automatically shifted to hug her shoulders. "I'm sorry. I've made a mess of things."

She shifted, and now she cupped his cheeks, holding him still so she could look at him. "I should have told you, but... I was afraid I'd lose you. I was afraid his name, his money and power..." Her voice trailed off and her hands dropped to her sides. "In the end, he still got his way."

"Maybe." Kade shrugged. "We'll figure it out."

"I love you. I always have, from the very first moment they handed you to me. Your father could have offered me a million dollars. Ten million. It didn't matter. You were my own sweet baby. And look at you now."

He felt his skin flush but he dropped a kiss on her hair. "Now his will makes sense. He wanted me to take the Barron name one way or another. He set it up so I'd have to or lose everything."

"It's a terrible position to be in, but have you considered this?" She faced him and tugged nervously at the plackets of his shirt. "What if I had given you up?" He stiffened but she tugged to get his attention and continued. "What if he'd been single and we'd married? And one last what-if. What if I'd simply added his name to your birth certificate?"

His brow knit into furrows as he thought about her questions. The answer to each of her questions was the same. As if she recognized the moment he came to that conclusion, Rose added, "You would have been named Kaden Barron."

It was hard to argue or refute that.

Pippa woke up disoriented. Why had she slept on the couch? Then she remembered. Kade had come for dinner again. She glanced around but he was gone. She focused bleary eyes on the LED clock on the cable box and yawned. Gray light filtered in through the windows. Since it was only 6:34, that shouldn't have surprised her. Yawning again, she stretched and wondered when Kade had left. With that thought came panic.

Tangled in the light cotton afghan, she almost fell on the floor until she got her legs free. Since the night her mother caught them in the pool, she'd insisted he leave by midnight.

She surged off the couch. They'd been watching a movie and she'd fallen asleep leaning against Kade's side with his arm around her.

She grabbed her phone, thinking to text him. If he'd

stayed all night, she had to leave now before her mother arrived at the door. Yes, Pippa was an adult. Yes, she technically lived on her own. Yes, she should be able to do whatever she wanted. But. Millicent Duncan was a force to be reckoned with when she went on one of her crusades. And for some reason, whom Pippa dated and what she did with them was akin to a holy war for her mother.

An unread text caught her eye. It was from Kade with a 1:30 a.m. time stamp.

Hey sleepyhead. I'm home but wanted to thank you again for a great night. I enjoyed the burgers and chick flick. I'll call you soon.

Whew! He hadn't fallen asleep, too. Pippa knew her mother. She would have stayed awake as long as Kade's truck was parked out front. Pippa poured a glass of orange juice and slid onto a barstool at the center island. She needed to work on some grant requests today, and she should check with Kade about leads on horses to buy. That would be a good excuse to call him. That was her story and she was sticking to it. Her thoughts, as they often did, returned to that *swim* she and Kade had shared. She'd felt wicked and risqué making love to him outdoors like that, even if the yard was secluded, with a tall privacy fence and a screen of landscaped trees and foliage.

Her parents hadn't been home that night. Their charity event should have kept them occupied until midnight. Her mother was a society maven who lived for such glittering affairs. Had Pippa daring to entertain a man brought them home early? At least she and Kade had finished, even though they'd been caught—Pippa laughed as a term she'd first read in a historical romance came to mind. *Déshabille.* Oh, yes indeedy. She and Kade had definitely been undressed when her mother caught them.

She saluted the empty room with her orange juice. "Here's to striking a blow for freedom."

Thirty minutes later, she eased her Highlander out of the garage and down the driveway. If she stayed home, her mother would come to harangue her about Kade's presence. With her laptop, Pippa could work anywhere. She considered going to the neighborhood coffee shop. They made a killer white chocolate blended iced coffee and had fresh-baked pastries, but it would be one of the first places her mother would look, should the woman decide to stalk her.

Inspiration hit. She'd head to the downtown library. She could park in the Barron Tower garage, her vehicle out of sight, and then walk up the street to the library. The place was huge, with free Wi-Fi and lots of out-of-the-way places where she could set up to work without interruption. She doubted her mother would think to look for her there. Even if she did, the chances of being found were slim to none.

A few minutes later, when she pulled into the parking garage and found a space, she realized the library wouldn't be open yet. Her stomach grumbled and she really wanted coffee too. The Colcord was a block away. The hotel restaurant opened early—and had free Wi-Fi.

She grinned. Perfect. She could get a real breakfast and lots of coffee while getting some work done. Then she could walk off breakfast going to the library. She loved it when a plan came together.

Shouldering her laptop bag and her purse, she locked her car and headed for the ground level. When she reached the restaurant, only a few tables were occupied. The hostess, noting her messenger bag, led Pippa to a table tucked back in a corner and showed her where the electrical plug was located.

Firing up her computer, Pippa surfed through some sites with lists of available grants. She made notes while eating, then savored one last cup of coffee. At the library, she worked diligently, forcing her mind away from Kade. They were friends. With benefits. Weren't they? She wasn't sure and she didn't want to ask him.

She emailed requests for more information. Wrote proposals and forwarded them to Carrie for editing and proofreading. She caught herself doodling Kade's name so when an email from Carrie popped up, she needed a break. After reading Carrie's invitation, she was ready to call it a day. She packed up and headed back to the garage to retrieve her car.

Pippa didn't even have to go home. Her best friend had suggested a movie, complete with appetizers and cocktails followed by dinner. The theater down in Moore had balconies and director suites with reclining chairs, VIP service and drinks. She didn't even care what movie—anything to keep her mind off Kade.

If she was lucky, Carrie would suggest a sleepover.

Pippa laughed. Who was she kidding? All she had to do was mention her mother and Carrie would insist she spend the night. Yes, distractions were good things to have. So was a best friend.

Eight

Pippa settled into her chair and took a sip of her white wine. She'd nibble, have the one drink then switch to a Diet Coke for the duration of the movie. Her cell phone vibrated. She let it go to voice mail, thinking it was most likely her mother. When it vibrated again, indicating she had a voice mail, she scrambled to get it out of her back pocket without spilling her drink. Her mother refused to leave messages and the only other person who might be calling her on a Saturday evening was Kade. Scrolling through the missed calls, she saw his name. She couldn't listen to the message fast enough.

"Hey, Pip. I'm on my way back from Davis and just hit Norman. I know it's late notice but I wondered if you might like to get together tonight. Call me."

With wide eyes, and her heart pounding way too fast,

she remembered to breathe. "Kade," she whispered to Carrie. "He's in Norman headed north and he wants to do something tonight."

"Call him!" Carrie commanded. "There's an empty seat next to you. While you're talking to him, I'll go reserve it. Hurry."

"You don't mind?"

Laughing, Carrie stood. "I'm sticking around for the movie but we came in separate cars. You're a big girl. You can go do whatever."

Fifteen minutes later, Kade had a Coke and a bucket of popcorn and was sitting next to Pippa as the credits began to roll. Moments after that, his hand curled around hers and he gave it a little squeeze. He leaned over and whispered in her ear.

"I know I'm horning in on your girl time. Thanks for letting me. After the movie, I'd like to take you and Carrie to dinner."

Pippa turned to whisper back and he caught her chin in his other hand. His lips descended on hers. His tongue traced the seam of her lips, teasing them apart until she opened for him and he could deepen the kiss. She kissed him back and when the movie started, they were both a little breathless.

"Are you sure?" she asked softly, waggling her eyebrows in what she hoped was a suggestively teasing way.

"Yeah. S'long as it's a short dinner."

A laugh burst out and she clapped her hand over her mouth to the hissing sounds of disapproval from other theater patrons. Pippa slunk low in her seat but eventually straightened and found herself enjoying the movie despite her awareness of the very attractive man sitting next to her. At the end, she held his hand and was a little teary-eyed in a that-was-so-romantic way.

Out in the parking lot, the three of them debated where to go for dinner. Carrie stared pointedly at Pippa. "Where is the last place your mother would stalk you?"

The question got a narrow look from Kade, but Pippa wasn't ready to discuss that situation with him. A sudden thought struck. "Cattlemen's."

"Ooh! I haven't eaten there in years," Carrie admitted. She glanced at her watch. "It's Saturday night. How long do you think the line will be?"

"There aren't any events in town," Kade said. "Probably not too bad by the time we get there."

"Let's go!" Carrie was off and running toward her car.

Kade's prediction proved to be right. They didn't have to wait long and after giving their orders to the waiter, Carrie didn't waste any time getting straight to her intentions to embarrass Pippa.

"Did you know Pip had *the* biggest crush on you in college?" she asked with a sly glance at Pippa.

She blushed and glowered. "Carrie," she warned.

"No. Really?" Kade squeezed Pippa's thigh gently and cut his eyes in her direction. Did he just wink at her? She settled back against the booth, leaving the discussion in his hands.

Carrie nodded like a bobblehead doll. "Really and truly. Why do you think she was hanging around the barns all the time? She was a sociology major, for goodness' sake."

Kade leaned away so he could turn to face Pippa. "Sociology? Yeah, I knew that. All the guys on the rodeo team just figured she was studying the flirting habits of the American Cowboy."

Carrie snorted iced tea out her nose. "Dude. Don't make me laugh when I'm taking a drink. That's so rude."

He handed her the bandanna perpetually tucked in his back pocket. Carrie blew her nose into it and announced, "I am so keeping this now."

Pippa used her napkin to hide her smile. She was right—Kade had been letting her know he planned to tease Carrie. That was wonderful as far as she was concerned. Carrie was her oldest and best friend and there was no way Pippa would let a man come between them. The fact that Kade wanted to include her bestie was one more reason she was attracted to him.

Carrie leaned across the table and said in a stage whisper, "I like him."

Laughing, Pippa said, "Of course you do."

"No, you don't understand. I *really* like him." Carrie settled back on her side of the booth and turned her attention to Kade. "Are there any more like you at home?"

Kade went still. Once upon a time, he would have laughed at Carrie's question and said something along the lines that no, he was an original. He would then most likely follow up with the information that he was an only child. But he wasn't. Not anymore. He had five brothers now. Not that any of them were available.

"No," he said eventually, and left it at that.

"Shoot," Carrie groused. "That's too bad." She flashed an impish smile. "Maybe I'll just wait until Pip gets tired of you…" She didn't finish the statement, blowing him a kiss with a suggestive wink instead.

Finding Pippa's hand, Kade squeezed it to pull her attention to him. "Will you, Pippa?"

"Will I what?"

He liked that she sounded breathless. "Get rid of me?"

His gaze remained glued on Pippa. The pulse point on her neck throbbed and she wasn't breathing. When she did inhale, her breasts rose and fell, drawing his gaze for a brief moment. He returned to her face, watching for telltale clues about her thoughts. Her lips parted and her tongue curled over the bottom one, drawing it into her mouth. Kade took that for an invitation.

Dipping his head, he zeroed in on her lips. He intentionally kept the kiss gentle—almost chaste, in fact. When he released her mouth, he whispered, "Glad you want to keep me around."

Their food arrived, disrupting the romantic interlude. Carrie kept the conversation light as they ate. While contemplating dessert, Pippa swiveled on the bench seat to face him. "We need to talk," she said, voice solemn and expression serious.

Was there a hint of worry as well? More curious than concerned, Kade asked, "Okay?"

"I need your help."

"Okay."

She startled at his quick agreement. "You don't even know what I'm asking of you."

He lifted a brow and waited.

"Okay, then. Well, two things. First, I need a date."

"Sure."

She straightened her shoulders as if she was about to say something unpleasant. "Do you own a tux?"

He didn't. The last time he'd worn one, he'd rented it. If he and Pippa had a future, maybe he should consider buying one, but he had the distinct feeling something else was up. "Why?"

"Because Chase is cosponsor of the fund-raiser for my foundation—a big gala at the Barron Hotel. It's black tie and all the movers and shakers will be there." Her words tumbled out in a rush, like a confession, and she wouldn't meet his gaze.

Ah. There were tricky undercurrents in her statement. The easy one was that she was concerned he'd feel out of place. He was a working cowboy, not upper class like her. Still, he knew which fork to use and standing on the periphery of the Barron family for the past several years had exposed him to the real and the fake in local society. It was kinda cute that Pippa didn't want him to feel uncomfortable. At one time, he might have taken offense, but he wasn't that Indian kid wearing worn boots and patched jeans anymore.

That left the other aspect of her admission. She'd been working closely with Chase, and given the current situation where he and the Barrons were concerned, how difficult would it be for him? Could he stand up to the scrutiny and the innuendos? He could, but why would he put himself in that situation?

He made a snap decision, one he might come to regret but the hopeful look on Pippa's face was too much to resist.

"I'll get one."

Pippa's eyes widened and her mouth gaped open for a few seconds. Then she beamed. "You'll come with me?"

"Yeah."

"Well…okay then." She sounded so relieved, as though she knew she'd put him on the spot.

She'd mentioned two items on her agenda. "What's the second thing?"

"Oh! Yes…well." She inhaled and squared her shoulders again. "I want to hold a second fund-raiser. This one more about the people Camp Courage will be working with. I want the big-money sponsors to have the chance to meet our clients."

"Seems like a good idea."

"Do I have your permission to hold it at the Crown B?" The request came in a rush of words and she bulled ahead. "I mean, it makes sense. We could show them how the riding therapy works. The sponsors would have the chance to meet and interact with some of the kids, the veterans, all types of people we want to help, and do it in a casual setting."

Surprised, he stared at her. "Isn't that a question you should ask the Barrons?"

"But you're the ranch man—" She snapped her mouth closed as a look of panic washed over her face.

It seemed as though she'd just figured out the situation. Kade stuffed away his anger. If he walked away from the Barrons, he'd be leaving the Crown B behind.

And if he didn't make a decision soon, one would be made for him, according to the terms of the will.

"Oh, Kade... I... I didn't stop to think." Pippa glanced at Carrie, who was intently studying them both. After a not-so-covert exchange of looks, Carrie excused herself with a lame excuse, leaving him alone with Pippa.

Her hand hovered over his arm before she jerked it back. "I'm so sorry, Kade. I... Things... I forgot." She hung her head, looking miserable.

He didn't want Pippa to feel bad. The situation between him and the Barrons... He persisted in labeling them that, refusing to call them what they were—brothers, even if only half. That didn't stop the three older ones from accepting the twins. They'd all made overtures, reaching out to him. He was the one resisting. Pulling Pippa into the middle of this wasn't fair.

"You should ask them," he finally said.

She dropped her gaze. "It was sort of Chase's idea. He's been incredibly helpful. He even offered to recruit Deacon for an appearance. Having Deacon Tate, country music's hottest star, there would be a real draw, and Chase said he wasn't afraid to play the cousin card." She kept her eyes on the hands she'd clasped in her lap beneath the table as she continued. "Chase said the hotel is donating everything for the gala. I'm pretty sure Chase is picking up the tab on the sly but it's just so wonderful because all the donations will go to the foundation."

Kade gritted his teeth. Why was Chase so involved in Pippa's stuff? Was it a way to get to Kade? Was Pippa in on the Barrons' machinations? A flash of anger constricted his breathing.

Pippa stopped speaking and the tension between them ratcheted up a notch in the ensuing silence. "I'm sorry," she whispered, voice catching. Her hand landed lightly on his forearm where he'd braced it on the table. "I'm incredibly insensitive."

He had to know. "Did they put you up to this?" He asked the question between gritted teeth. Her sharp inhalation and the tremor in her fingers before she jerked her hand back told him what he needed to know before he even turned his head to look at her. He'd hurt her—and he regretted it.

Scrubbing a hand through his hair, Kade examined his emotions, something he usually avoided. Lashing out at Pippa wasn't the answer to his dilemma. He closed his eyes, saw his grandfather's disapproving face. Instead of facing the situation like a man, he was running away like a kid with a case of the "Don't wannas." He should apologize but the simmering anger clogged his throat. Instead, he skirted everything by asking, "So when is this fancy deal requiring a tux?"

Pippa winced, her gaze flicking up to his before sliding away. "Next month?"

The month flashed by. While Kade spent time with Pippa, the easy camaraderie they'd previously shared was strained. Kade admitted the disconnect was his fault, but he didn't know how to fix things. He also avoided interacting with any of the Barrons, including Chase's wife, Savannah. Savvie was like Kade's little sister, but she was a Barron now. Since none of the wives—known for their meddling—had gotten involved, he suspected their husbands hadn't told them about the terms of the will.

Kade hoped he could put things to rights by escorting Pippa to her gala. He bought a Western cut tuxedo and, like a teenage boy taking the prom queen to the dance, he went to work on the rest of the evening. Carrie, as if she sensed what he was doing, informed him that Pippa's gown was *pewter and Oklahoma blue*—whatever that meant. He finally gave up and asked. She informed him, "Gray and a blue the color of the state flag."

Why couldn't Carrie have just said that? She went on to explain that he should coordinate his tux accessories to match and no, this wasn't prom, so no flowers.

He hated shopping but found a formal vest with silver threads running through it and snatched it without even looking at the price tag. He wasn't about to mess with a bow tie so he added a black bolo tie with pewter tips and a large turquoise slide in lieu of the bow. He also made arrangements for very special transportation.

When the big night finally arrived, just as he was about to walk out the door, Pippa called him in a panic.

"I don't know what to do," she all but wailed.

"Breathe, Pip. Tell me what's wrong."

"Mother. I'm so mad I could spit. I just got back from the hairdresser and she met me at the door. *I expect you to do your duty*, she says. *Everyone is gathering here prefunction for cocktails and you will be here to act as hostess.*" Kade was impressed at how well Pippa imitated her mother. "She hates my foundation and she's hijacking my party just to be contrary. I don't have time for this command performance of hers. I have so much left to finish with the event itself and she must have set this up weeks ago but she chose *now* to drop this little bombshell on me? *Argh!*"

"So what you're saying is that your mother planned this party for two hundred of her closest friends and she expects you to play hostess?"

"Yes."

"Are these people also invited to the deal at the hotel?"

"Yes."

"Okay."

"Okay? Okay? That's all you have to say?" Her voice rose in pitch.

"You aren't breathing, Pip. What time does your mother's thing start?"

"Six."

"What time does the other thing start?"

"Eight."

"What can Carrie and I do at the hotel so you can relax for a bit?"

"I can't…you… Carrie…" He could almost hear her jaw snap closed through the phone. "Let me think. Carrie has a copy of my list. If she's dressed early, she can deal with the hotel on the final room setup and menu."

"Can I handle that for you if she can't?"

"You'd do that for me?"

"Sure. I was just on my way out the door anyway. I'll be there early just hanging around. If I pick you up at seven, you'll have an hour to make nice with your mother's friends, who are your potential donors. When I get there, I'll whisk you away, giving you enough time to regroup and be ready to make your entrance at the hotel."

Pippa didn't speak for a long moment. Then she said, "Kade?"

"Yeah?"

"I *love* you."

He went very still, like prey sensing danger. Except he knew she didn't mean what she'd just said. It was a throwaway line meant to show her relief and appreciation. But a part of him kind of liked the idea of her saying it for real. Which was crazy.

"Anything to help, hon. Email me the list. I'll make sure everything is good and then I'll pick you up at your parents' at seven."

Kade drove into Oklahoma City and parked near the Barron Hotel. He'd arranged for the horse-drawn carriage to meet him there. The round-trip to the Duncan's home and back to the hotel was about three miles on mostly quiet streets. The carriage was for her grand entrance. After the event, he planned to drive her home in his truck. He checked his watch and had more than enough time to deal with arrangements before the ride to Pippa's.

Tonight was the culmination of so many of Pippa's plans and he wanted everything to be perfect for her despite the last-minute wrench her mother had thrown into things. The hotel event director was an efficient woman who eyed him speculatively. He was saved when Chase and his wife, Savannah, arrived. Chase took over the preparations, leaving him alone with the woman who knew Kade well.

"So…anything you want to tell me?" Savannah went straight for his jugular.

"About what?"

Her brows lowered over squinted eyes. "The brothers have been really closed-mouthed about you of late, despite all of us wives bugging them."

"You should take it up with your husband, Savvie."

"Is it true?" Her gaze was both speculative and knowing.

"What?"

"Don't go all…*man* on me, Kade."

"I am a man."

"Argh!" Savvie threw her arms up and almost clipped Chase on the chin as he walked up behind her.

"Whoa, kitten. I'm the only one who gets to frustrate you like that." He kissed the back of her neck before looking at Kade. "You look good. What time are you picking up our hostess with the mostest?"

"Seven. Her mother did this thing."

Chase grimaced. "Ah yes. The inestimable Millicent. I dodged that bullet for us, Savvie. You can thank me later. When we're alone."

"So," Savvie continued, ignoring her husband. "Are you going to tell me or what?"

"Tell her what?" Chase asked.

"That's what I asked," Kade said.

"You guys! Stop it. I want to know."

Kade exchanged a look with Chase, one he hoped the other man understood.

"So, you serious about Pippa?"

And that was not the direction he expected Chase to take, but Kade could run with this diversion. "I'm just helping her out with foundation stuff. She's picking my brain since I did all that research about therapy riding when Cord was hurt."

"Uh-huh." Chase sounded totally unconvinced. "Will you offer the use of the ranch for her next event?"

Kade wasn't sure what Chase meant. Keeping his expression carefully blank, he said, "It's not up to me to give permission about how the Crown B is used."

"Uh-huh."

Now Chase sounded…what? Skeptical? Smug? Whatever it was in his voice, Kade wasn't going to play this game. "Since you seem to have things well in hand here, I'm going to pick up Pippa before her mother drives her completely nuts."

He walked out of the ballroom, well aware that both Chase and Savvie were staring holes in his back. One thing at a time. And here and now, his one thing—his only thing—was Pippa Duncan.

Nine

Cars clogged the street but the horse-drawn carriage stopped in the one available spot at the end of the Duncans' driveway. The coachman set the brake on the carriage wheel and let the reins go slack. The dappled gray draft horse patiently flicked an ear as his driver glanced back at Kade. "Big party."

"Yeah. Sorry. I'll have to extract her from this mess."

The man chuckled. "No worries, sir. Dozer and I will be here."

When he got to the front porch, Kade tugged his jacket into place and rang the doorbell. And waited. After several minutes, he knocked. When he still didn't get an answer, he tried the knob. The door wasn't locked. As he started to push, the door was jerked open and he faced the haughty Millicent.

"May I help you?" She arched one perfectly plucked and dyed brow and frowned.

"I'm Pippa's escort tonight. I'm here to pick her up."

"She's not ready to leave yet." Millicent did her best to shut the door on him.

Kade wasn't having any of that. He shouldered his way inside. Politely, despite Millicent's arrogant attempts to stop him. His frustration boiled to the surface so he leaned down to whisper in her ear, "I don't give a damn about appearances so making a scene is no skin off my nose."

The woman huffed out a breath, but stepped out of his way. He pasted a smile on his face and worked very hard to keep his cool. Pippa's mother really was a piece of work. Luckily, he was tall enough to see over most of the crowd milling around. He pushed through the throng until he found Pippa pinned in a corner of the dining room. Millicent dogged his footsteps like she was afraid he might steal something.

He caught Pippa's eye and almost smiled at her relieved expression. He edged through the four women surrounding her and used his most charming smile as he addressed them. "Excuse me, ladies, but Pippa has a gala to attend."

Pippa snatched the hand he held out and he extracted her smoothly. He caught a few whispered comments as they threaded their way back to the front door.

"Who's that?"

"Handsome, isn't he?"

"I didn't realize Pippa was seeing someone."

"I think that's one of those Barron boys, but I don't recall which one he is."

Speculation, snideness and honest curiosity coated the expressions and remarks of those who uttered them. Pippa looked pale and her eyes showed a tightness Kade was all too familiar with. She had a migraine coming on. Part of him wanted to sweep her into his arms and get the hell out of there. He hoped that once he got her away from these people and out in the open air of the carriage, she'd be able to relax.

"Do you have whatever you want to take with you?" he asked, keeping her tucked close to his side.

"I need my evening bag. It's in Dad's office. Here." She tugged on his hand, veering to the left. She opened French doors and slipped inside. The room was wood paneled, dark and furnished with antiques. Pippa grabbed the small beaded bag on her father's desk and they headed back into the crush.

Kade bulled his way through. He'd been kidding about two hundred of Millicent's closest friends. But there were probably close to that many crammed into the Duncan home. He and Pippa made it to the door, but stalled as more people arrived. She had to acknowledge the newcomers for a few minutes and then they finally escaped.

He led her to the sidewalk. That's when she realized there was a white carriage waiting for them. Kade had arranged to have blue ribbons and silver roses for decorations and he was glad he'd gone to the extra trouble and expense. Pippa stopped in the middle of the sidewalk, her hand pressed over her heart, eyes wide and glistening.

"Oh, Kade," she sighed. "You did this for me?" She bounced up on her toes and kissed him. "This is the most romantic thing ever," she whispered in his ear.

"Your carriage awaits, princess."

Pippa insisted on being introduced to Dozer. The coachman was happy to oblige. By the time Kade lifted her into the backseat, she was smiling and the tightness around her eyes had disappeared.

"This is just... I'm..." Pippa laughed and the sound went straight to his chest.

Kade *liked* it when she laughed and he really liked it when he was the one putting a smile on her face. But he shouldn't. He wasn't in the position to get involved. Not until he figured out his own messed-up life. Dozer took off at a rousing walk, his big hooves clopping rhythmically on the pavement. The bells on the draft horse's harness jangled a merry counterpoint.

"I can't believe you did this, Kade."

Slightly embarrassed now, he sought to change the subject. "You look beautiful, Pippa." Color flooded her cheeks, which seemed to make her eyes bluer. Her long, wavy blond hair had been twisted up in some fancy style that his fingers itched to undo. And her dress... *wow.* It was the color of storm clouds, the skirt swirling around her legs. The top was covered in beading and sparkles the color of the Oklahoma sky on a perfect autumn day. She wore little makeup, her freckles vibrant against her flush. Small and colorful and delicate, she reminded him of a ladybug.

As if on impulse, she leaned closer and kissed his cheek. "Thank you for making the rest of my night perfect."

"You're welcome, ladybug." Riding in the back of the carriage, with Pippa snuggled up next to him, holding her hand, he realized, yeah, she was right. The night was perfect.

When Kade had walked into the room, Pippa had never been so glad—and relieved—to see anyone in her life. And bless him, he'd taken one look, figured out what was going on and gotten her out of there with minimal fuss and bother. And he'd even hired a horse-drawn carriage for a quiet ride through Heritage Hills and then downtown to the Barron Hotel. She would be arriving at her fund-raising gala in style.

While slowly unwinding from the stress of her mother's cocktail party, she was still nervous about the event. "Did you—"

"Chase was there with Savannah. I left everything in his far more capable hands."

She laughed again, and the tenseness in her muscles dissipated. With it went the last vestiges of her headache. She wouldn't have to medicate tonight. That meant she could have a glass of wine and eat some of the wonderful refreshments prepared by the Barron Hotel's five-star kitchen staff.

Kade gently squeezed her hand, then raised it and kissed its back. "You are an amazing, talented, caring, beautiful woman, Pippa. Tonight will be everything you hope because you're the one who put it together.

You'll make lots of money for Camp Courage and we'll get started with looking for a location and for horses."

"You're really good for my ego, Kade Waite."

"I try, ma'am." He winked then kissed her—carefully—so he didn't mess up her lipstick.

For the next ten minutes, they simply sat close together, holding hands, enjoying the sounds of the horse and carriage. As they passed landscaped yards, she caught the scents of honeysuckle and mimosa, both sweet but just different enough to distinguish. New-mown grass added a note of green that hid the scent of hot motors and car exhaust.

Kids ran out to wave at them like they were a parade consisting of one float. Pippa practiced her princess wave, much to Kade's amusement. She didn't care. She felt like a princess tonight and had her very own Prince Charming by her side. In the distance, the sound of traffic intruded. They were close to downtown now and they'd be arriving at the hotel soon.

"What time is it?"

"A little after eight. You are arriving fashionably late."

She blanched. "Oh, no! I should have been there to greet—"

"Shh, Pippa. You have others there to greet the early arrivals. I was informed that you need to make an entrance so that's what we're going to do."

She made a disgusted face and rolled her eyes. "Carrie."

"And Chase."

"They're in cahoots." She thought about her best

friend and the Barron twins. "Did you know that she and Chase dated in high school?"

He gave her a look that said volumes, like *How would I know that? I didn't go to your private high school.* She wanted to bite her tongue. "Everyone figured they'd end up with each other eventually. Carrie told us we were nuts. Turned out we were. Still, those two together are far too devious for their own good!"

She very carefully laid her cheek on Kade's shoulder. She didn't want to smear her makeup on his black tux jacket. "You see, Carrie was a female version of Chase. They were all about the opposite sex and never settling down." She raised her head so she could look at him. "And do you know how crazy happy he is with Savannah? I never thought he'd fall so deeply in love with anyone."

"Yeah, weirdly enough, I think Savannah feels the same way about him."

Pippa realized she was wearing a soft smile when she saw it reflected in Kade's dark eyes. Street lamps were glowing and stars were twinkling in the sky. A crescent moon peeked over the top of the downtown skyline. She sat up straighter as they stopped at the light at the intersection of Park Avenue and Broadway. When it changed, Dozer trotted into the circular drive in front of the Barron and joined the queue of cars lined up for the hotel's valet parking.

Looking around, Pippa was amazed. Lots of people had self-parked and were walking into the hotel. "So many people…" She couldn't have hidden the wonder in her voice even if she'd wanted to.

"Why wouldn't there be? This is a good cause, Pippa. An amazing cause. You've tapped into lots of people's soft spots. Even those without deep pockets."

While she'd worried Kade might feel out of place at a black-tie affair, the man sitting beside her looked nothing but proud—of her and to be with her. And she thought she might have fallen just a little bit in love with him.

Kade watched her work the room—not from afar but at her side. Once they arrived and he'd handed her down from the carriage, she'd been all but swallowed by the crowd. Somehow, they'd remained together, most likely due to the fact that she clung to his hand like it was her lifeline. He'd anticipated finding a place on the periphery from which to watch. Now he stood next to her while she visited with guests, her face animated and all but glowing with the passion she held for her cause.

He believed in her cause. He'd first looked into therapy riding programs after Cord Barron had been injured in an accident on an oil rig. Active in the OSU Outreach Riders, Kade had worked with disadvantaged kids but had no clue there was so much more to a therapy program. Physically and emotionally challenged children and adults, military veterans, even recovering drug addicts and felons had all benefited from association with horses. Kade would do everything he could to help Pippa see her dream come true.

Currently, she was talking to a neurosurgeon and his wife. Kade stood slightly behind her and schooled his face so he didn't smile whenever she rocked back to lean against him. He'd figured out that she touched him when she was feeling anxious or needed support.

"What do you think, Mr. Waite?" the doctor's wife asked. "Will this program have an impact on autistic children?"

Kade scrambled to catch up with the conversation he'd mostly tuned out. "I can't say for sure, ma'am. The research I've done indicates that kids can and do connect with the horses. I know when I was at OSU and we brought in foster kids for field trips, they really got into it. I'm just sort of the horse consultant in this deal."

The woman looked thoughtful, then interrupted her husband as he was about to reply. "Get the checkbook out, Oscar. And add a zero to the amount we discussed earlier." She turned a megawatt smile on Pippa. "I think this is a wonderful idea and I wish you much success. Please let me know as soon as you open. I'd like to sign up my grandson."

Pippa looked startled then regrouped. "Of course! I'll be in touch with you, Mrs. Amadi, just as soon as we're up and running. Thank you."

Dr. Amadi had done as his wife requested and when Pippa looked at the check, she almost choked. Kade was afraid he'd have to slap her on the back to get her breathing again. She sucked in a breath and added, "This is beyond generous. Thank you both so very, very much!" She shook the doctor's hand and when she offered her hand to Mrs. Amadi, the woman hugged Pippa.

"No, my dear, thank you. I hope you can reach my grandson."

"We'll do our very best, Mrs. Amadi!"

The couple moved away and Pippa sagged against Kade. She waved the check in front of him. "Look," she gushed.

He did a double take. Twenty thousand dollars was a lot of zeros. "Carrie's working the donation table, right?" Pippa nodded, still stunned by what she held in her hand. "Let's take her the check and then I want to dance with my date."

Carrie had a running total for them and Pippa was all but floating as he took her into his arms on the dance floor. The band was playing something soft and romantic and he liked having her head on his shoulder as they swayed in time to the music. The gala had garnered well into six figures and Kade regretted his paltry thousand dollar donation. It had seemed like a lot when he signed the check—especially when comparing his bank account to others' in the room.

The people attending this gala were the movers and shakers of Oklahoma society. He noted the knot of men at the end of the bar—Cord Barron, his father-in-law, J. Rand Davis, and three other energy tycoons. Their conversation was intense. The governor held court at a table on the edge of the dance floor. The OU football coach occupied one table, the OSU coach another. A couple of professional basketball players and their dates shared the floor with Pippa and him.

Kade didn't fit in with these people. He was just a rancher—on a spread that wasn't even his. But it could be. The back of his neck prickled and as he turned Pippa in a slow circle, he searched for the cause. He found the Barron table. All of them but Cord sat there with their wives. Jolie, Cord's wife, was taking a turn at the donation table with Carrie. Clay, Chance, Chase and Cash all watched him.

His brothers. With the Barron name, he could be sitting at that table. He could add zeroes onto the end of a number as he wrote a check for charity. Kade missed a step and caught the hem of Pippa's dress with his boot.

"Sorry," he murmured.

She gazed up at him with worried eyes. "Are you okay? You look like you've just seen a ghost or something."

Yeah, or something all right. He smiled, turning his back on the men with the same eyes as his own. "Naw. Just clumsy."

Her grin was full of mischief as she looked at him. "Thank goodness I'm not the only one."

When the song ended, Carrie grabbed Pippa and insisted she take a turn at the donor table. At loose ends, Kade headed to the buffet. Cord had joined his brothers and now they all sat there watching him. They'd remained true to their word—for the most part. They hadn't approached him about the terms of the will. They'd given him space, dealing with him only when necessary about the ranch or this deal with Pippa. They weren't like their old man—*his* old man. At least he didn't think so.

A short, stout woman, wearing a black dress with so much beading Kade couldn't figure out how she could move in it, nudged him with her elbow.

"Here, young man. Take this." She shoved a plate laden with a bit of everything on the table at him. He grabbed it out of self-preservation. "I can't possibly navigate with a plate and a libation." She held up a crystal flute full of bubbling champagne.

Like a tugboat chugging through a harbor full of cruise ships, she navigated to a table near the one occupied by the Barrons. When they arrived, he placed the plate next to one full of desserts and just managed to hide his amusement as she leaned her head back to look up at him.

"My goodness, you are a tall one. I never could keep all of you straight. Now which one of the Barron boys are you?"

Ten

After the party wrapped up, with Pippa's announcement that they'd raised $243,211 for Camp Courage, she laughed about Kade's encounter with the elderly matron. He'd dodged the woman's question simply by introducing himself. He'd received a sharp-eyed assessment in return, and by the time he escaped, the woman had been distracted by something else.

"Mrs. Mayweather is notorious for picking out one handsome man and making him dance attendance on her. She'll be talking about you for days with her garden club cronies." Pippa leaned back against the leather seat of his pickup. She rubbed at her temple and Kade wondered if she was aware of the action. "My parents didn't come."

That she felt hurt was evident in her voice. He

reached over, took her hand and gave it a little squeeze. "Less drama."

That startled a little snort from her. "True, that." She tilted her head to look at him as the truck rolled to a stop at a red light. "Mother is something of a drama queen. Sadly, she managed to keep some potential donors away too."

That made him angry but he held his tongue. Instead, he offered encouragement as he continued driving toward the Heritage Hills neighborhood. "You'll figure a way to reach out and touch them."

"I hope so. I'm only about halfway to my goal."

"You've been applying for grants."

"Yes, but those can take a year or more and none of them are huge. I'm looking at them for an infusion of operating funds after the first glow wears off. This is a long-term program. I need to find a steady source of revenue."

As they approached the street where her parents' house was located, Pippa sat forward, pulling against the seat belt. "Looks like the party is still in full swing."

The disappointment in her voice was as strong as her previous hurt. "How 'bout you sneak in, pack a bag and come back to the ranch with me. You can sleep late. I'll fix you breakfast and then we'll take a ride."

Pippa's expression lightened. "Perfect! Go up a block and park. I have the code to the back gate."

Kade did as he was told, then helped her out of the truck and escorted her to the gate. She rolled her eyes at him, which he was able to see due to the overhead security light from the neighbor's yard.

"I think I'm safe walking this half block."

"Probably."

"You could have waited in the truck."

"Yup."

"Kade…"

"Pippa…"

She laughed then and smothered it against his chest. "We need to be quiet. If Mother catches us, we'll never get away." After she keyed in the security code for the gate used by the yard care crew, they tiptoed across the pool area and slipped into the guesthouse.

Pippa left him in the living room. One lamp lit the area. She dashed upstairs without switching on additional lighting. When she returned, she wore jeans, flipflops and an OSU T-shirt, and pulled a little wheeled suitcase behind her. She paused near the door and grabbed a pair of Western boots from the shelf of an antique hall tree and passed them to Kade.

She peeked out from behind the curtains. "The coast is clear. Let's go."

When they were safely back in his truck, Pippa was giggling like a kindergartner and he couldn't stop the grin spreading across his face.

"Thank you," Pippa said, her voice fervent as he put the truck in gear and pulled away from the curb.

"For what?"

"For…this. For tonight. For making me laugh. For having faith in me."

He glanced at her as he turned the corner at the end of the block. "You're doing a good thing, ladybug."

"I know. And I want all the money possible to go to

the program itself. I'll keep doing the administrative side with volunteers for as long as possible. I won't take a salary. I can live on part of the interest from my grandmother's trust. The rest of it will be used for day-to-day expenses. With enough donations, I won't have to touch the principle."

"Is that why you live in the guesthouse?" He'd wondered, given the frequent animosity between Pippa and Millicent.

She stretched out her legs and leaned back against the seat with a yawn. "That's a big part of it. I don't have to pay rent or utilities and it's convenient. I have budgeted for things, should I move out." She turned her head and smiled in his direction. "And the perks are pretty good." She waggled her brows.

By the time he hit the north side of the city, Pippa had dozed off. He thought about what she'd said, about living off the interest of a trust fund, about setting up a charity foundation that didn't have administrative expenses so all the money could go for good.

Kade had worked his whole life. He'd joined baling crews in junior high, and in high school, he'd traveled with harvesting crews. In between, he'd trained horses and competed in rodeos. Even with scholarships, he'd worked his way through college and had graduated debt-free. He compared his life to the Barrons and other rich kids he'd gone to school with. All things considered, the Barrons had turned out fairly normal.

He thought about the ranch and the money that would come with it. He thought about what he could contribute to Camp Courage. And he thought about Pippa.

She hadn't given any indication that she wanted to take their relationship beyond what it was—basically friends with occasional benefits. He liked her. A lot. And he enjoyed spending time with her, in or out of the bedroom. Did he want to take whatever they had to the next step? Did she?

Kade already had way too much weighing on his mind. Given his situation, starting a serious relationship with a woman like Pippa was foolish. She belonged with someone like one of the Barrons. Not him, despite his DNA. She was a princess, he was…a simple cowboy. Pippa deserved someone with more class, someone brought up the way she'd been. That sure wasn't him. Money didn't make the man, but having it smoothed out the rough edges. If he accepted the Barron name, he'd have more than enough to give him a veneer. But that wasn't him, and never would be. He was comfortable being Kaden Waite. Kaden Barron? Not so much.

He glanced over at the sleeping woman. She'd never shown a snobby bone in her body but would she consider something more with him—with the ranch manager and not the ranch owner? Would he be able to give her all the things she was accustomed to on his salary? If he walked away from Cyrus's deal, he'd have to find another job, another place to live. She wouldn't want to give up her dream of the therapy program. He wouldn't expect her to go with him.

Sudden money did bad things to people. He'd watched it happen to members of his tribe who'd come into oil money. He'd been raised to work with his hands. With the kind of wealth the Barrons had, they didn't need to work. But they did. All of them. He hadn't considered that until now.

"You're thinking so hard you're giving me a headache, Kade."

"Sorry. Thought you were asleep."

She chuckled and made a face at him. "What'd I say about thinking?"

"Oh, right. Sorry." But he wasn't, especially when she reached across the center console to touch his arm. He dropped his right hand from the steering wheel and twined his fingers with hers.

"No, you aren't." She squeezed his hand. "Thank you again. For tonight. For…this. It's weird, because there's absolutely no reason I should feel this way, but it's like a weight's been lifted from my shoulders." She gazed out through the windshield. "I love coming out here. I mean, I enjoy living in the city but coming out here where I can really see the stars and it's so quiet… It's peaceful, y'know?"

A wry grin tugged at the corner of his mouth and he let it blossom. "Yeah, I know. But I'm a small-town boy and grew up on a farm. Even Stillwater, while I was there for college, was a big city to me."

"I like that you're a country boy, Kade."

She squeezed his hand again and something eased in his mind. A warmth he didn't want to examine too closely filled him. "Well, this country boy likes the city cowgirl sitting beside him."

Pippa remembered to breathe. Tingles danced across her skin as she gazed at his handsome profile. She knew he didn't like to dress up, yet he had. For her. And that caused more tingles. Kade was a real country boy. He worked hard for a living and didn't she just love the way his rough hands felt against her skin? She shivered and Kade glanced at her.

"Cold? I can turn the AC down." He reached for the controls, still holding her hand. She tugged it back.

"No, I'm good."

He flashed her a wicked grin and her breath caught in her chest. "Yeah, you are."

Blushing furiously, she ducked her head and did her best to hide the very pleased smile spreading across her face. "Not as good as you," she mumbled under her breath.

She settled back in her seat and watched Kade from the corner of her eye. The glow from the dashboard instruments bathed his skin in gold. She'd only pretended to doze on the drive partly because she was exhausted from talking all night and craved some silence. Not that Kade was all that talkative. Her other reason had been so she could simply sink into the pleasure of watching him without his knowing. Pippa got such a kick out of it, she decided to do it at every opportunity.

It was only after his expression had sobered and then he'd looked…not forlorn but deeply saddened. That's when she spoke up. She'd had a wonderful—if tiring—night and having him by her side had been the boost she needed. When he'd appeared at her parents' house, she'd felt such relief and she'd been struck by how handsome he looked—rugged and sexy and very, *very* male.

The carriage waiting outside had been the perfect

touch, and was beyond romantic. She'd worried, briefly, when they entered the hotel ballroom, but he'd stuck with her, supporting her and aiding where he could. He stood back and let her shine, and that was such a rare trait in most of the men she knew that she viewed it as a precious gift.

"Have I mentioned how wonderful it was to have you beside me tonight?"

Kade laughed and nodded. "Yeah, once or twice. Trust me, I'll figure out a way for you to pay me back."

He slowed the truck and turned onto the road leading to the ranch. They passed between the fieldstone pillars that supported the metal sign—Crown B Ranch Established 1889—arching over the drive.

The interior of the big house was dark as they drove past. Security lights left soft pools of fake moonlight scattered around the exterior. Pippa caught the crunch of gravel under the truck's tires as the vehicle left the brick-paved drive for the utility road leading to the ranch office, barns and the houses occupied by other ranch workers. As Kade pulled up in front of his house, a light activated by a motion detector went on.

Kade came around to open her door and help her down before grabbing her bag and boots from the backseat of the king cab pickup. They hadn't really talked about the circumstances of his birth since his original confession and without thinking, Pippa blurted, "If you decide to stay, will you take over the big house?"

Her blunt question was a testament to her exhaustion. Appalled by what she'd said, she turned to him, eyes wide. "I'm sorry. That… I… Not my business!"

His expression was inscrutable as he turned away from her and climbed the steps to the porch. Kade unlocked the front door and held it open for her to precede him. She scuttled past, keeping her face averted. Pippa was positive she'd insulted him somehow.

After locking the door, he headed toward his bedroom. He stopped in the doorway. "No," he said without looking at her. "I'd keep this house. Does that… I don't know. Upset you? Disappoint you?" He passed into the darkened room without waiting for her answer.

Pippa tossed her purse on the boot bench next to the door and hurried after him. In his darkened bedroom, the ceiling fan created a cool breeze to wash over her skin. A lamp occupying one of the bedside tables flicked on with a bluish glow, chasing the dark into the corners. She loved the stained-glass shade that cast those soft colors.

Leaning her shoulder against the doorjamb, she watched Kade place her suitcase on top of his dresser. Her suitcase was heavy but he exerted no effort lifting it. He dropped her boots next to the dresser then started stripping out of his tux. He meticulously hung the jacket on a thick wooden hanger. The turquoise bolo tie went on a rack on the back of the closet door. The fitted vest with its woven threads of silver was placed on a second wooden hanger. Pippa had never truly noticed before but Kade was a precise housekeeper. His home was lived in but everything had a place and was put there.

His fingers tangled with the tiny studs on the tux shirt. She went to him and brushed his hands away as her smaller and more nimble fingers worked the gray pearl and metal studs out of the buttonholes. She saw a plastic box on top of the dresser and dropped the studs into it before going to work on his cuff links.

"Of course not, Kade," she said quietly without looking up. "I don't even know why I asked that stupid question."

He shrugged and the lift of his muscular shoulders parted the plackets of his shirt even more. His sculpted chest had a fine feathering of hair a shade lighter than the black hair on his head. She placed a kiss in the center of his chest before dropping the links in the box with the studs and stepping away. Kade caught her hand.

"It wasn't stupid, Pippa. You live in a mansion."

She snorted and rolled her eyes. Making sure her voice was light and teasing, she said, "I live in the guesthouse of a mansion."

"Okay, fine. You grew up in a mansion. So did the Barrons. Their house in Nichols Hills is every bit as fancy as your parents'. And the big house here could be on one of those home decorating shows. You know them. You know how they live."

He swept one hand wide to encompass the bedroom. The rustic king-size bed was formed from pine logs. The bedside tables and dresser were well worn and carried a patina of age while not being antique. The armchair and matching ottoman were covered in distressed leather and looked comfortably lumpy. The whole place was similarly furnished. "This isn't fancy. *I'm* not fancy, Pippa. I wasn't kidding when I said I was a country boy. At the end of most months, we had more days than money. I've worked—worked hard—for everything I have. I don't know what it's like to have the kind of money they do, that you have."

Kade walked away and sat down on the wooden blanket chest at the foot of the bed. He toed off his polished black boots and held them up. "I bought these at Langston's outlet store. Tonight, the Barrons were wearing custom boots that cost what some people make in a month."

Pippa wasn't sure where he was headed with this so she stayed where she was despite the very visceral need to go to him, to touch him. He pushed off the chest and popped open the fastenings of his slacks. Stepping out of them, he crossed back to the closet, passing so close that had she leaned forward his arm would have brushed her breasts as he walked by. She resisted the urge but dang the man was sexy, even standing there in an open shirt, black knit boxers and black socks.

Emerging from the closet, Kade mirrored her earlier posture by leaning a shoulder against the door. He'd shed both shirt and socks. "My point, Pippa, is this. I've never had anything. My idea of a manicure is using a pocket knife to clean the dirt from under my nails and washing my hands with Lava soap. I'm a working cowboy with a fancy title that doesn't mean crap when the herd needs moving, there's a rough calving or there's a fractious mustang to break to the saddle."

He scrubbed one hand through his hair and breathed hard for several moments. "I don't know what it's like to have that kind of money. I don't *want* that kind of money. And you're the kind of girl who—" Kade chopped off the rest of the sentence, then dipped his chin and stared at his bare feet rather than continuing to look at her.

She blinked, a puzzled look on her face. "I… I'm not following, Kade. Are you breaking up with me?"

Eleven

Pippa's question stung but it also made Kade think. Did they have a relationship serious enough that they'd actually have a breakup? He considered.

They were dating—and sleeping together. She was intent on getting her therapy riding program set up and he was helping her with that. She would come to the ranch and they would ride or they'd laze around the pool at the big house. Being with her made him feel settled, made him want things he hadn't considered before. Knowing she was coming out to the ranch, or he was headed into town to spend time with her made him work a little harder, a little faster, so he could finish that much sooner.

She was important to him but he didn't love her. And he wasn't the kind of man she would ultimately love and marry. He was a man who spoke his mind and he had. He'd been honest with her. And with himself. He was a working man. Pippa was an heiress. She lived on a trust fund and set up foundations to help those in need. She moved in society circles where formal clothing was something hanging in their closet, not rented from the bridal store. Her kind of people lived in mansions and drove expensive cars they paid cash for. That kind of money was foreign, yet as close as his signature on a bunch of legal papers. That kind of money could define a man.

Kade didn't realize he'd been silent too long until Pippa jerked her head around, hiding her face from him as she surreptitiously swiped at her cheek with the back of her hand. "It's too late for you to drive me back to the city. I'll sleep on the couch and you can take me home in the morning."

She thought the answer to her question was yes. His fingers wrapped around her biceps as she stepped away and he tightened his grip until she stopped. "Do we have something to break, Pippa?" Damn but he sounded needy.

She wouldn't look at him but she answered him. "I don't know. I thought we had something special."

Air whooshed out of his lungs as relief washed through him. He was treading dangerous ground but the feel of his heart hammering in his chest made him say, "We do, Pippa. We do have something special."

Then she was in his arms, her tears dampening his chest. He held her close, stroking her back and kissing the top of her head. "I'm sorry, ladybug. I'm sorry. I didn't mean to hurt you. It's just… You deserve a man who's better for you."

"Shut up. Just shut up, Kaden Waite. That's not true. You *are* a better man!"

Her words steadied his pulse rate and he could breathe without the hard hitch in his chest. After a few minutes of just standing there holding each other, her breathing steadied as well. He helped her undress and then they climbed into bed. He wanted to make love to her but the dark circles under Pippa's eyes reminded him of how exhausted she must be. Midnight was a couple of hours past and dawn would arrive all too quickly.

He settled on his back with Pippa curled to his side, her palm warming the spot over his heart, her head on his shoulder. "Sleep, ladybug."

"Are we okay now?"

"Yeah, sweetheart. We're good."

Kade lay awake long after Pippa drifted off. Eventually he fell asleep, but woke up early with Pippa still in his arms. His mind couldn't let go of their conversation. Her question last night had thrown him, and made him wonder if everyone thought he'd take over the big house if he accepted the terms of Cyrus's will. Of course, if he didn't agree, it wouldn't matter. He'd be packing everything he owned into his old truck, because the truck he normally drove belonged to the ranch fleet, and moving away. He had no idea where he'd go. It wasn't like he'd started sending out résumés or anything.

Pippa stirred beside him and he inhaled the ginger orange scent of her long hair. Sleeping with her in his arms brought him more peace than he figured he was entitled to at present. She made him forget, even when they weren't having amazing sex. Just her presence soothed the ache in his chest.

He was leaning over to kiss her good morning when she violently shoved against his chest and jolted upright. Kade jerked his head back just in time to avoid getting clocked on the chin. Pippa's legs got tangled in the sheets and she would have fallen face-first on the floor if he hadn't grabbed her.

"Pippa?"

She had her hand pressed over her mouth and she looked a little green. He got the sheet unwrapped and then she was off the bed and bolting for the bathroom. A few seconds after the door slammed shut, he heard the unmistakable sounds of heaving. Yeah, time to vacate the room and start coffee. He wanted to help but his gut reaction told him Pippa would not appreciate the intrusion.

She hadn't appeared by the time the coffee finished dripping into its carafe. Kade gulped down a cup and when she still hadn't emerged, he tapped softy on the bathroom door.

"You okay, ladybug?"

He heard a muffled yes.

He waited for more, got nothing. "Can I do anything to help?"

"Grab my clothes?"

"I can do that."

He took her suitcase from the top of his dresser and tapped on the door again, which opened just wide enough for him to pass the bag through. Pippa stayed hidden behind the door so he couldn't even get a glimpse of her. The door closed with a soft snick and he heard the lock turn. That didn't bode well.

When she appeared ten minutes later, she'd showered and gathered her wet hair into a ponytail. He fought the urge to kiss the tip of her freckle-sprinkled nose. Shadows bruised her eyes and she was pale beneath the freckles. He preferred her like this—no makeup, hair natural, in faded jeans and a soft shirt, but he could tell just by looking she was sick.

"You okay?"

Pippa lifted one shoulder and huffed out a hitching breath. "Sorry. I don't normally wake up needing to throw up. It must have been something I ate."

"That's not good."

She nodded morosely. "It would be very bad if something was wrong with the food at the gala. I'll have to call Chase and ask if anyone else got sick."

"I'm sorry, bug. Want some coffee or juice?"

She closed her eyes and shook her head. "No. Still queasy. I'm sorry about today. Maybe you should just drive me home."

He shook his head. "Do you really want to deal with your mother feeling like this?"

"Good point."

"You can either go back to bed or I'll set you up on the couch. You rest and I'll take care of some work this morning. Then, if you feel better, we'll ride or something this afternoon. Sound like a plan?"

Her smile was tentative. "Yeah. Thanks." She closed

her eyes and swallowed hard. "Do you have any ginger ale or crackers?"

Kade had both. He went to the kitchen and grabbed a box of crackers and a can of soda. While she ate a couple of crackers, he put ice into a glass and poured the liquid into it. He watched as she nibbled and sipped, was glad when color returned to her pallid cheeks.

He did have some work he could do but he was hesitant to leave her after he made her a comfy nest on his couch. He made sure the sleeve of crackers and the glass were within easy reach, along with the TV remote and her phone. Pippa snuggled against the pillows he'd brought from the bedroom and he tossed a light throw over her. Her smile was warm and her eyes had lost their tense look.

"I can stay with you," he offered.

"No, you have things to do. Go take care of them. Maybe I'll feel like lunch and a ride when you get back."

He left, still reluctant. Kade hadn't invited her out to spend the night and following day just so he could work. Still, he recognized that her illness had embarrassed her and she wanted a little time apart as much to regroup emotionally as recuperate physically.

His first stop was the office, which was locked up tight. Not unusual for a Sunday. He let himself in and went to his desk. A stack of messages awaited his attention. Flipping through them, he decided there was nothing demanding his immediate response.

He grabbed a six-wheeled ATV parked outside and headed toward the barns. He paid a visit to Imp's stall. The yearling nickered and moved toward him. The straw on the floor was fresh; the colt had been fed and given fresh water. Kade grabbed the lead rope and halter hanging next to the stall and slipped them onto the horse. Leading Imp outside, he turned the colt out into the large corral next to the barn.

That done, he checked the other stalls. All was well. Dusty appeared during his inspection and jumped into the ATV's passenger seat, intent on accompanying Kade on the rest of his rounds. He drove out to the nearest pastures to check other horses and then herds of cattle. Sunday was a rest day for the cowboys on the ranch.

When he got back, a lone figure with blond hair blowing in the wind leaned against the corral fence watching Imp play. He parked the ATV and walked toward her as Dusty raced to her side for petting and attention.

When Kade reached her, Pippa favored him with a smile and she reminded him of daisies. "You must be feeling better."

"I am. I'm fine now. What would you like to do?"

Things low in his belly stirred to life but he fought the urge to suggest going back to bed. Instead, he said, "Let's go on a picnic. We'll ride out to the lake, take a swim, eat." Then he couldn't resist. He waggled his brows. "And see what happens."

Pippa laughed and waggled her finger. "I see what you're doing here."

"And?"

"I didn't bring a swimsuit."

Kade's cheeks stretched with his grin. "Good. Then I know what's going to happen!"

"Thank goodness!" Pippa grabbed his hand and pulled him toward his house. "I'm hungry. What are you going to feed me?"

And didn't that just put all sorts of ideas into his head.

No. Just...no. This conversation could not be happening. Pippa stared in horror at her best friend. "Wash your mouth out! I've always been careful. I'm on birth control for goodness' sakes."

After a month of intense meetings in the aftermath of the gala, Pippa'd planned for a day of shopping fun and lunch at Cadie B's with her BFF. They occupied a shady table on the patio. She'd wanted time with Carrie but this conversation had not been on the agenda.

"You might be but there's always the possibility for an oops moment. Let's look at the evidence." Carrie raised her index finger. "You wake up nauseous every morning."

"It's just that stomach bug going around." Of course it was. The virus had even made the nightly news. Except she'd been living on crackers and ginger ale from the time she woke up in the morning until just before noon. Then she felt fine. The first few days had been intense, though. Upon waking every morning, she'd had to run to the bathroom even though she made sure she ate nothing before bed.

Carrie put up another finger, as if counting things off, and stared at Pippa's plate. "When was the last time you ate sauerkraut? I've known you since we were five, Pip, and you have never, ever eaten a Reuben sandwich.

You inhaled that one. And you ate kraut on your bratwurst at the baseball game the other night. I sat there and watched you. And then you wanted another one. You don't like hot dogs, much less bratwurst. You get pizza or Frito's Chili Pies when we go to the ballpark. Even Kade noticed."

"He did not!" She scowled at Carrie then blanked her expression to one of unconcern. "What's the big deal? So I had a craving."

"Precisely. Think about why women have cravings." Carrie raised a third finger. "And other than being a little stressed over setting up the foundation, you haven't acted PMS-y in well over a month."

"I don't PMS." She didn't. Much. But Pippa also couldn't remember her last period. Stress. It was just stress. Besides, she'd never been all that regular. That's why she'd first gone on birth control and the whole not-getting-pregnant thing was just a side benefit, especially since she and Kade had been spending so much time together. She hadn't missed a pill since they'd started dating.

Raised eyebrows lost under her bangs, Carrie shook her head, looking for all the world like a disappointed parent, though with a humorous twist to her mouth. Pippa was all too familiar with the real thing. Leveling a look at her, Carrie was insistent. "Of course you do. You forget. We roomed together at OSU. Trust me, you PMS. Not as bad as me, but you get witchy. It pains me to say this, but sweetie, you are in denial."

"No, I'm not. This is ridiculous, Carrie, and I'm not talking about it anymore. Subject closed. I set aside today to shop and spend time with my best friend, not get a lecture." Pippa pushed to her feet and snagged her purse from where it hung on the back of her chair. Fighting a wave of dizziness, she walked, with as much dignity as she could summon, to the door.

She was still wobbly when Carrie caught up to her. "Pip? You okay?"

"Migraine coming on," she muttered. "I don't have my meds with me. I…sorry, Care Bear. I need to get home."

"C'mon. I'll walk you to the parking garage." Luckily, they weren't far and once Pippa made it into the gloomy interior, she felt a little better. She said goodbye to Carrie, climbed into her Highlander and cranked the air-conditioning after punching the ignition. She closed her eyes, waiting for the next wave of precursors, only there were none—no sparkles, no tunnel vision, no pain tuning up to the beat of her pulse. Idling in the shade of the garage, she realized she'd simply misdiagnosed the problem. Her dizziness wasn't a result of the debilitating headache she'd expected, just more symptoms from that erratic stomach flu.

Feeling better, she decided to head toward her favorite coffee shop. Even if this was a very tiny migraine, the infusion of caffeine would help. She had her favorite e-reader in her purse. She'd find a quiet corner, drink an iced coffee and read for a bit. Between her tummy troubles and the stress of meeting with high-powered people regarding grants for Camp Courage, it was no wonder she was queasy.

Pippa was in no hurry to go home. Her parents were

in Barbados. They'd embarked on a two-week cruise with friends on their yacht and would be home in a few days. In the meantime, no one would be waiting for her. Honestly, she'd enjoyed her mother's absence. Since the night of the gala, Pippa had received either the cold shoulder or scathing accusations.

Still, she faced eating dinner alone and found the idea unappealing. She considered calling Kade to see if he wanted to come into town and hang out with her. They could watch a movie. Or baseball. She didn't care. She just wanted company—his company. And with her parents away, he could spend the night.

She passed one of the big chain drugstores and a little voice told her to stop. Pippa kept driving. For two blocks. Then she whipped around and returned to the store. She stood in the aisle for almost twenty minutes before making her selection.

And that's when she realized she'd be spending tonight alone—until she figured things out.

Twelve

The next morning, wrapped in nothing but a towel after her shower, Pippa stared at the test stick in her hand. She immediately grabbed the other two brands of pregnancy test and read the instructions. Took them both. And got the same result.

This. Could. Not. Be. Happening.

She sank onto the closed lid of the toilet and cried. How could she be pregnant? She splashed her face with cold water, staring at her reflection in the mirror. She didn't know what to do. Crying hadn't helped. Holding out hope that all three tests were false positives was grasping at straws. Breathing through another wave of panic, she grabbed her cell phone and scrolled through the contacts to find her doctor.

Able to get an emergency appointment, she dressed

and headed to the doctor's office. After the nurse ran a series of tests, took her blood pressure and weighed her, Pippa sat on pins and needles for two hours, refusing to leave the waiting room until she had confirmation and an explanation. The nurse finally escorted her into Dr. Long's office. She knew the moment she saw the doctor's face. Sinking into the nearest chair, she fought another onset of tears.

Dr. Long pushed a box of tissues toward her. Pippa pulled a handful and blew her nose. "So, it's true."

"Yes."

She'd always liked Dr. Long. The woman was calm, deliberate and blunt when the situation called for it. Even as her heart sank, she appreciated the doctor's directness. "Two questions." At the doctor's nod, she said, "How did it happen and what do I do now?"

Dr. Long leveled a look at her. "I presume you got pregnant the way most women do."

That called for a glower and she tossed one the doctor's direction. "Okay, d'uh. But I've been on the pill for three years."

"What other drugs are you taking?"

"I…several. You know I have severe migraines. Dr. Nevin is my neurologist." Pippa frowned. "And I've doubled up recently because…well…lots of stress."

"That likely explains how. Some of those drugs affect the efficacy of birth control pills."

"Why didn't you warn me? I would have made Ka— my partner use other precautions."

"Three years, Pippa. And how many sexual relationships have you had in those three years?"

She opened her mouth to answer, then closed it.

Dr. Long's severe expression softened. "This is a recent development, I'm guessing?" Pippa nodded. "The young man I saw you with at the gala?"

"Yes."

"As to your second question, I can't tell you what to do. You have options and you know what they are. The one thing I need to know is whether or not you plan to carry the pregnancy to term. If you do, then we'll need to adjust your medications to prevent…complications."

"Complications? You mean like—" Pippa swallowed down a surge of panic. "Like birth defects?"

"Among other things. We'll need to find alternatives to managing your migraines."

Pippa sat quietly, considering. Options. Keep the baby. Give it up for adoption. Abortion. Part of her wanted to run away and just deal with it all by herself. Maybe tell Carrie for moral support but her parents… Oh, Lord, her parents. They would go ballistic. And Kade. What would Kade do? They'd only been close for a matter of months. She had to tell him. And she knew in her heart of hearts that he had a right to help her make the ultimate decision.

"Pippa?"

"I need to think, Dr. Long."

"I figured you might." The doctor scrolled through her computer records. "You'll need to get with Dr. Nevin to begin a step-down on the migraine medications. He won't want you to quit cold turkey. And you didn't ask, but you're about eleven weeks along. We're looking at a January due date."

"Okay," Pippa said with no emotion. Dr. Long looked concerned. "No. I'm fine. Okay, not so much." The soft laugh that escaped bordered on hysterical. "I'll be fine. I'll get through this."

"I know you will, Pippa."

Sitting in her car in the parking lot, Pippa fought the urge to call Carrie so she had a shoulder to cry on. But she couldn't tell Carrie before she told Kade. Or her parents. She dug her phone out of her purse. Should she call him or text him? Not to tell him but to set up a time to talk. Or maybe she should just drive out to the ranch. Yes, that was the ticket. No sense making him fret while she drove out there, right?

Depending on traffic, the drive could take between forty-five minutes and an hour. Pippa caught herself speeding several times. She didn't normally have a lead foot but it was as though the weight in her chest had sunk all the way into her foot. She didn't *want* to get to the ranch fast. Part of her argued that she should turn around and just go home. But she couldn't do that.

Pippa did her best to concentrate on driving but thoughts tumbled through her mind. What would Kade do? They'd really only just begun their relationship. She cared for him a great deal and she suspected she was in love with him. That didn't necessarily mean that she loved him. To her, being *in love* was the butterflies and silly grins, the yearning, the dreaming, the flash of heat. Loving someone over the long haul meant so much more. Being honest with herself, she could admit she'd dreamed about their relationship becoming more.

Friends with benefits, lovers, a couple, and then marriage and babies. Wow, had she messed up that timeline.

Another thought intruded. How would the pregnancy
affect the funding of her foundation? Would she be able
to participate fully in Camp Courage? She had too much
going on. Too many decisions.

And she had no one to blame but herself. Pippa had
been so cocky and sure that they were covered in the
birth control area. Glancing at the speedometer, she
eased off the gas pedal again. She glanced at the sign
announcing the next exit and cringed. Two more exits
and then she'd almost be at the ranch. She had to tell
Kade but she had no idea what to say.

"Um, hi, Kade. You're going to be a father." She
grimaced. "Yeah, no." She thought some more. "Hey,
Kade, we need to talk. You know when I said I was on
the pill? Well, about that…"

She continued talking to herself until she turned off
the section line road and drove under the arch announcing the ranch's name. Cattle grazed on both sides of the
winding drive. As she neared the big house, she could
see the smaller pastures closer to the barns. Horses
nibbled the early summer grass. She didn't see Kade's
truck at first and relief warred with dread. She didn't
think she could maintain her equilibrium if she had to
wait much longer.

As she passed the big house, Pippa saw Big John un-
loading groceries from his Explorer. Dusty was dancing around him until the dog saw her Highlander. He
chased her all the way to the ranch office. Kade's truck
wasn't parked there or at his house, either. She had to

focus on breathing around the knot in her chest. She parked at the office but before she could get out, she caught a flash of white in her rearview mirror. Kade's truck. He was driving along one of the ranch tracks.

Steeling herself, she got out and waited for him. Dusty, as if sensing her mood, leaned against her leg rather than his usual jumping and frolicking to get her attention. Her hand dropped to his head and she rubbed the dog's ears.

Kade pulled up but didn't park. The passenger window glided down and he leaned across the seat to call to her.

"Hey, ladybug, did I forget something?" He looked confused but pleased. Pippa wondered how long that expression would last.

"No. I guess I should have called. I know you have work—"

His expression morphed to one of concern. "Work can wait. What's up?"

"I…we need to talk, okay?"

Now he looked blank. "Yeah, sure. Get in. We'll drive over to the house."

That was probably for the best. He reached across and popped the door open for her. She shooed Dusty away, climbed in and shut the door.

"You okay, Pip?"

She didn't answer. She didn't know what to say. They covered the short distance in silence and she waited in the truck while he got out, came around and opened the door for her. "Pip?"

"Inside, okay?" She couldn't look at him, knew the look on his face would kill her.

In the shady interior, he offered her a cold drink, which she declined. She wouldn't sit, either. She couldn't. There was too much nervous energy zinging through her body to settle. All the words she'd planned to say, the ones she practiced on the drive fled as she looked at him. She opened her mouth and two words came out.

"I'm pregnant."

Kade didn't breathe. Surely he hadn't heard that right. But as he looked at her, he saw the truth. And everything snapped into place. The morning sickness. The odd things she'd eaten on their dates. The way her face had rounded, grown softer.

"Mine?" The question was out before he could stop it and regret followed on its heels at the look on her face. He hurried to add, "Of course it is. How far along are you?"

She frowned even after he answered his own question. "Almost three months. And you know it's yours."

"We'll get married. My child is gonna have my name." He blurted that without thinking too, and in a much harsher voice. It was true though. His child would carry his name, would know who his—or her—father was.

"No." Anger flushed Pippa's cheeks.

What did she have to be mad about? He was offering to make an honest woman of her, to give their child a name. Then he wanted to kick himself. His mother's name had been good enough for him. It still was. He lowered his chin and rubbed the back of his neck.

"That came out wrong, Pippa." He glanced at her. "Will you marry me?"

"No." Again with the quick denial.

He felt his own anger surge. "Why not? Am I not good enough for you? Is my name not good enough for our baby? Would the Barron name be more suitable?"

Pippa blanched and Kade felt like the worst SOB. Maybe he carried more of his father's DNA than he thought. He reached for her. "I didn't mean that, Pip. I…this…"

"Yes," she said and he brightened for a moment. Then she continued. "It is…this. I just found out this morning. Got in to see my doctor. She confirmed things. I'm sorry, Kade. I didn't plan this. I… I'm not one of those women who would trap a man like this."

Kade rocked back, stopped himself and reached for her. She jerked away but he went after her. Being as gentle as he could, he reeled her in until he could wrap his arms around her and she was leaning into his chest. "I know, ladybug. I know that."

"I…" She sniffled. "I didn't know my migraine medication would mess with the birth control. I didn't want this to happen."

Cold dread filled him. Was she thinking of doing something drastic? The idea hadn't even occurred to him. Yeah, having a wife and baby would be a huge change but the idea that she might terminate the pregnancy? He stiffened.

Pippa leaned back and stared up at him. "What?"

Her eyes widened and filled with panic. "No. Don't you dare ask me that. Just don't. I can't. I won't. This baby is mine!"

Relief replaced the dread as an adrenaline rush tingled in his extremities. "Never, sweetheart. I would never ask that. I was just… I was afraid that's what you wanted. When you said you wouldn't marry me, that you planned to—"

Her hand covered his mouth, silencing him. "Don't even say it, Kade. Just don't."

"I won't, Pip. Please, come sit down. Okay? We'll talk."

She nodded so he walked backward, drawing her with him until his calves bumped into the couch and they sat. He kept her in the loose circle of his arms and let her find a bit of emotional balance. He needed to find it too. Damn. He was going to be a father. He started to grin.

"It's not funny," Pippa huffed.

"No," he agreed. "It's not. But it is pretty freaking amazing." His enthusiasm shocked her, if her expression was anything to go by. "Marry me, Pip."

She shook her head. "Still no."

"Why? If you're planning—" His breath seized again. "You aren't giving our baby away, are you?" Oh, hell no. He'd fight her every step of the way if that was her plan.

"No. I hadn't really even considered adoption. It's just…your proposal isn't sincere, Kade. It's a knee-jerk reaction. You don't love me."

She had him there. He cared about her but love?

What did he really know about love? Still, she was carrying his child and he had a responsibility to them both. "I won't let you deal with this alone, Pippa. I'm in for the long haul."

Kade placed his hand over hers where they cupped her stomach. He had the feeling she wasn't even aware she was doing that. How long would it take before he could feel his child move there? He chuckled, realizing he knew nothing about human pregnancies. Horses and cows? He was an expert.

"Are you laughing at me?"

"No, ladybug. At myself." He started to ask her about marriage again but she cut him off.

"The answer is still no, Kade."

"Fine." His abrupt reply got a startled blink from her and he used her momentary surprise to pull her into his lap. "I'm not going anywhere. I want to marry you, to give our child my name legally. I want to take care of you both. Fair warning—I'm not backing down on this. My father…wasn't one. Not to me, anyway. I won't follow in his footsteps."

Her gaze narrowed and he braced for her next denial. She surprised him when she said, "We don't know each other well enough to get married. We have no choice when it comes to being parents."

"Then let's get to know each other better. We'll keep dating. We'll see where things go. Will you agree to that?"

Suspicion crept into her expression. "It's not that simple, Kade. What's the catch?"

He kissed her pursed mouth before she could avoid him. "No catch, ladybug."

Not much of one anyway. He was determined to wear her down—which, judging by her dubious reaction, wouldn't be easy. They would be married before his child came into the world or his name wasn't Kaden… And then reality slapped him in the face. Because at the root of everything, he was no longer sure exactly who he was.

Thirteen

When he came to Pippa's house, Kade always parked on the street. Then he'd walk up the drive, avoiding the main house, to the guesthouse where Pippa lived. The whole place reeked of luxury. Living around the Barrons should have insulated him from this kind of wealth. Except the Barron brothers didn't flaunt theirs. Not exactly. They were used to obscene amounts of money yet at the same time, they lived mostly normal lives. They lived with the power and money but they didn't throw it in people's faces. Unlike Pippa's parents.

Kade still smarted over the first time he'd arrived at Pippa's invitation for a pool date. Her mother was something else, and every interaction he'd had with the woman since just reinforced his initial appraisal.

He pushed through the ornamental metal gate and

headed to Pippa's door. As he approached, raised voices coming from the pool area caught his attention.

"How could you!" Millicent Duncan's voice was as shrill and grating as a screech owl. "What are we going to do, David?"

He could picture the woman wringing her hands, a gesture Kade had seen often enough since he and Pippa had been together. He didn't want to eavesdrop but depending on where they were sitting, he couldn't approach Pippa's door without drawing her parents' attention. He hesitated, taking cover behind some bushes.

"She can always go to a clinic." Pippa's father had a deep voice that carried in the still evening air. "Or we could send her to Europe and place it for adoption after the birth."

A softer voice vibrated with anger. Pippa's. Kade knew it instinctively. He also knew what her father meant by "going to a clinic." They wanted her to abort the baby. *His* baby. Without conscious thought, he charged toward them. No one noticed him. Tensions were running too high. He halted, a potted tree screening him from the three.

"I'm not doing either of those things," Pippa insisted as she stood. She wasn't shouting but her voice carried clearly now. "This is the twenty-first century. Single women have babies all the time."

"Not our daughter," David Duncan snarled.

"But that's the problem, isn't it?" Millicent turned toward her husband. Kade caught her face in profile and the disgust in her expression halted him in his steps. "She *isn't* our daughter."

Those four words were followed by a stunned silence. Face white, Pippa stared at her mother. "What is that supposed to mean?"

Millicent tossed back the remains of the martini in her glass. "You aren't stupid, Pippa. What do you think it means? I didn't give birth to you. Your father is sterile. Our attorneys arranged a closed adoption and we paid your birth mother for you. Twenty thousand dollars."

Pippa stood there, her face devoid of color and emotion. Kade remained frozen.

"That's why you wouldn't give me a detailed health record." Pippa's voice sounded stunned and hurt as she sank back onto her chair as if her knees could no longer support her. When she faced her mother, her eyes looked bruised.

"You are no better than the woman who gave birth to you. She couldn't keep her legs closed either. I want you out of here, Pippa. You aren't my daughter. You never have been."

"Now, Millicent…" David attempted to soothe his wife. "We can work this out to our satisfaction."

"Don't patronize me, David. It was bad enough that she wouldn't date within our circle of friends, and then she went slumming when she started going out with that…that…" Millicent sputtered, evidently too disgusted to finish her accusation. The woman pushed out of her chair and with posture so rigid she might break from the sheer tension, she returned to the house. Eyes straight ahead, she never noticed Kade standing there.

"Dad?" Pippa said. "I don't understand any of this."

"I don't understand how you could be so careless."

Her father's voice was coated in disappointment, and something harder, something colder that Kade couldn't quite pin down.

"I wasn't, Daddy." Pippa stretched her hand across the table reaching for her father's. The man jerked it out of her reach and Kade had to shove his hands in his pockets to keep from striking out at him. Instinct told him to wait. Assaulting her father was not the answer.

"You're pregnant, Pippa. It's rather obvious that you were careless." Mr. Duncan pushed back from the table, the metal chair grating on the terrace stones. "Your mother has a point. It will be best for everyone if you go somewhere else for a while. You can come back once you've resolved this situation."

Pippa had to snap her mouth shut and take several deep breaths before she could speak. "This *situation*?" Her palms protectively curled over her stomach. "I'm having a baby, Dad. Your grandchild."

Her father shrugged as if what she said was of little consequence. "You're young, Pippa. Take care of it, settle back into your role and your mother will eventually come around. This foundation thing should go on the back burner until Millicent can come to grips that you work with charity cases. While I understand your altruistic tendencies—you always were too soft-hearted for your own good—"

"My own good? Are you serious?" She was horrified. The man she loved, the man in whose lap she'd felt warm and safe, was turning out to be a total stranger. She'd never been close to her mother but her dad? He'd been her rock and now he was... Pippa couldn't breathe for a minute. He *wasn't* her dad. Had he ever loved her?

Her father looked bored. "This discussion is over, Pippa. You know what needs to be done. I'll make a reservation for you at the Barron Hotel. You can stay there until you can get a doctor's appointment to deal with this. Then you can move back into the guesthouse. I'll help you convince your mother—"

"But she's not my mother, is she?" The question was out of her mouth before she could stop and think. Just like he wasn't her father. "She was quite emphatic about that, *David*."

He sighed and blasted her with his "I'm so disappointed in you" look. Pippa didn't crumble the way she would have before this evening. In fact, she wasn't feeling much of anything.

"Don't bother with reservations." The coldly controlled voice came from the shadows behind the potted tree beside the terrace. Kade. She was out of her chair even as her father whirled to face him.

"Pippa has a place to stay—with people who care about her."

Kade strode over, all tall and strong and self-contained. His face held very little emotion but she knew that look. Inside, he was fuming, anger churning like hot lava. He came to her side rather than confronting her father. That was good. She let out the breath she'd been holding. She wouldn't put it past Kade to punch her father's lights out, and then she'd have to spend the night arranging bail for him.

"I'll help you pack up whatever you want to take,

Pippa." His big, warm hand on her shoulder was meant to convey support but now she felt hemmed in between these two determined men.

"She's not going anywhere with you, Waite. You're the problem here. Pippa's infatuation with you and your inability to control your base nature—"

"That's enough!" Pippa shook off Kade's hand. "I don't need this. Any of it." She marched toward the guesthouse without looking back, leaving the two men glaring at each other.

"Stay away from my daughter."

Kade laughed at the order, and the sound was chilling. "I thought you just admitted she wasn't yours. Is she or isn't she? Because if she's not your daughter, you have no right to dictate her life. Can't have it both ways, Mr. Duncan."

The sarcasm in his voice was so thick, Pippa would need a steak knife to cut through it. She sped up to cover the short distance to her front door. She fumbled with the knob and a moment later, warmth covered her back.

"Let me help," Kade said. "He headed inside, which is good. I'd have punched him in another minute."

The back door to the main house slammed, the sharp slap of wood on wood echoing in the deepening shadows. Pippa jumped. Kade didn't.

"I'm sorry." She didn't stutter and was glad for her self-control.

"For what, ladybug?"

"How much did you hear?"

"Enough." His arm curled around her waist and he

pulled her back against his broad chest. "Probably not all of it, but enough to know they hurt you."

"Are you angry with me?"

He stepped back and she missed his warmth. But he only moved far enough away so he could spin her around to face him. "Why would I be angry with you?"

"My parents aren't precisely...politically correct."

Kade snorted. "Especially not where I'm concerned." He brushed his knuckles across her cheek and ended with a gentle tap on the end of her nose. "But you should know, Pippa. No one gets to treat you that way. I don't care who they are."

His serious expression and the hard glint in eyes gone the color of frozen coffee belied his tender touch. Without thinking, Pippa reached up to cup his face in her palm. "They treat you awful."

"That doesn't matter. But understand, Pippa, I won't stand by and let anyone hurt you. I care about you."

"Why? Why do you care?"

"Because you're carrying my baby."

And there was the real truth, she thought. She thinned her lips in a disapproving frown and twisted away from him. He cared about her but he didn't love her. And truthfully, all that really mattered was the child in her womb. There were times when she was convinced that was the only reason he was with her. They had horses and the foundation in common. Was it enough? They really were from two distinct social strata and while that didn't matter to her, she suspected it stuck in Kade's craw. Then she remembered. He was a Bar-

ron, despite the way he'd grown up. He was the heir to
a fortune in land, horses and cattle. If he wanted to be.

She managed to get her door open this time and almost shut it in Kade's face but he was quicker than
she was. Choosing to ignore his presence, she flopped
down on the couch and rubbed at her temples. Kade
was there in a flash.

"Are you okay?"

What a stupid question. Of course she wasn't. She
was pregnant by a man who didn't love her, a man de-
spised by her parents, and oh, wait. She'd just discovered she was adopted and that her birth mother had sold
her for twenty thousand dollars.

"Let me rephrase that," Kade continued. "I know
you aren't okay, not after what happened out there. I
meant your head. Do you have a migraine coming on?"

Elbows braced on her knees, Pippa bent forward and
dropped her face into her hands. "No. I don't even have
a headache." She peeked up at him. "Yet." She sighed,
then flopped back, head against the couch. With her
eyes closed, she said, "What a mess."

Kade was smart enough to keep his mouth shut. They
sat in silence while she thought. Pippa knew her parents. This would all blow over if she just stayed out of
sight and kept her head down. Every other time she'd
disappointed them, that's what she'd done. Eventually,
they forgave her. They would this time, too, and when
her baby came into the world they would love her child
as much as she did. They would. They had to. They
were her parents.

Except they weren't. At least not genetically. She had

questions now. Lots of them. Who had her mother been? And her father? Did they have diseases or genetic defects that could affect her baby's life? She needed to find them. Talk to them. Get the answers to her questions. Except how was she going to do that? *Closed adoption.* She knew what that meant. All the files would be inaccessible until her father agreed to help. Did he draw up the papers or would he have had his partner do it? She'd call Leo in the morning...

"Do you want me to help you pack?"

Kade's voice pulled her out of her reverie. She opened her eyes and blinked rapidly at him. "Pack? Why would I pack?"

"I thought your par—" He cut off the word. "Didn't they tell you to leave and not come back until—" His jaw snapped shut. It seemed that she wasn't the only one having trouble finishing sentences and thoughts.

"No. Well, yes, but they didn't mean it."

He eyed her dubiously. "Sure sounded like they did to me."

"The last time Mother got this angry, she threw me out of the house. Dad moved me out here. I was a junior in college. This is my home. They don't really expect me to pack up and—"

A knock on the door interrupted her. Casting an I-told-you-so look toward Kade, she headed to the door. "See? Already forgiven." She opened the door to find her family's longtime housekeeper standing there, her fingers twisting the material of the starched, white apron she wore.

"Delores? What are you doing here?"

"I'm sorry, Pippa. Your mother sent me out here to…" The older woman's face crumpled and tears welled up in her eyes. "I'm supposed to watch you pack and leave so you don't take anything that isn't yours. I'm to get the keys from you." Delores glanced at Kade. "And I'm to call the police if there is any trouble."

Pippa's vision darkened and sparkles danced across the blackness. This wasn't a migraine, but lack of air. She couldn't breathe. Arms surrounded her, steadied her. Warmth at her back. Someone whispering in her ear.

"Easy, ladybug. You need to breathe. We'll deal with this." Kade murmured something else but she didn't understand—couldn't follow his words. He was speaking to the housekeeper. Then she felt a phone being pressed into her hand. "Call Carrie to come help. We'll get you packed and moved out tonight."

She followed his orders but by the time her best friend arrived, Pippa was too numb to help. Thank goodness for Carrie. For Kade. Even Delores. They found her luggage. Packed her clothes, her personal items.

"Furniture?" Kade asked.

Pippa ran her palms over the suede couch she occupied. She loved this couch. Had enjoyed picking it out on a shopping trip with her mother. Mother and daughter had had a lovely day—shopping, lunch, then more shopping followed by massages and mani-pedis at her mother's favorite day spa.

"I'm sorry," the housekeeper said. "Mrs. Duncan says the furniture belongs to the family, not to Pippa.

She can only take her clothes and the personal items Miss Carrie packed."

Pippa felt Kade's anger from where he stood behind her. At least she could feel something instead of the icy numbness that had gripped her since the housekeeper's earlier pronouncement.

"Okay," she murmured.

Kade came around the couch, helped her to her feet. "I'm taking you home, Pippa."

"Home?"

"With me. You're staying with me."

Her gaze found Carrie, who hovered nearby.

"That's a good idea, Pip. Go home with Kade until we get this figured out. I'll drive out to see you tomorrow, 'kay?"

"Okay."

Still in a fog, she allowed Kade to draw her outside, listened while Carrie fumbled with her keys. "Change of plans, Kade. I'll follow you to the ranch. Is it okay if I spend the night? Somebody can bring me back in the morning."

"Yeah, fine. What about your car, Carrie?"

"I didn't drive. I caught a cab. Good thing, since I don't want to leave her Highlander here."

Kade nodded curtly. "Understood."

Pippa was glad someone understood what was going on. She certainly didn't. She wasn't sure she would understand anything ever again.

Fourteen

Pippa stretched before opening her eyes. The bed beside her was cold but she'd come to expect that. Kade worked for a living and ranch chores waited for no one. She focused on her body, felt the wave of nausea. Sitting up slowly, she discovered a sleeve of crackers and a can of ginger ale on the bedside table nearest her. She'd read somewhere that eating a couple of crackers before getting up could help control the morning sickness.

She had three crackers and washed them down with the ginger ale. And almost immediately felt better. Who knew? Well, obviously Kade. The thought made her laugh, then she remembered that Carrie had followed them to the ranch the previous night. Her stomach clenched at the ugly memory. What in the world would she do now?

A soft tap at the door was a welcome distraction to her gloom-and-doom thoughts. Her best friend's face appeared in the doorway. "Hey, you. How do you feel?"

That was a loaded question. Pippa sat up and plumped the pillows behind her so she could lean against the headboard. She decided to answer honestly. "I'm not sure."

"Fair enough." Carrie joined her on the bed, sitting on the end, her back braced against one of the large pine bedposts. "Kade filled me in on the scene last night. Your mother is a royal—" She bit off the word. "Well, you know what she is. Any clue about what comes next?"

When Pippa shrugged, Carrie continued. "Kade wants you to move in here. I think that's a good idea. I mean, you can work on the foundation from here. And he'd previously offered to stable any horses you purchase before you get a place leased. Heck, given the way he's catering to you right now, he'd probably let you open Camp Courage right here!"

"So…" Pippa arched a brow at the other woman. "Your advice is to move in with the man who is barely my boyfriend."

Carrie stuck out her tongue. "Barely? Girl, that horse is so far out of the barn you'll never catch it. He's your baby daddy."

It was Pippa's turn to make a face. "I hate that term. Yes, he and I made a baby together. That doesn't necessarily make us a couple."

"It doesn't?" Kade's voice came from the threshold, startling her.

But she was quick to take up the gauntlet. "We're dating, Kade. That's all. At this point, I'm not even sure if we're doing that anymore." Pippa was determined to stand up to him. She was emotionally bruised and refused to let him run over her.

"We're going to be parents, Pip. You're having my baby. Carrie's right. You should move in here. In fact, we should get married."

"No!" Pippa was absolutely adamant. "We aren't having this discussion again. We are *not* getting married." She glanced at Carrie and held up her hand in a halting gesture. "And don't you start on me either. I refuse to get married just because I'm pregnant. In fact, I should leave here now. Can I stay with you, Carrie? Just until I can find a place of my own."

Carrie's gaze bounced between Kade and Pippa. "Um…sure. I guess."

Pippa climbed out of bed and grabbed some clothes. "I'm leaving, Kade. Just stay away from me until I figure out what to do."

Kade was a patient man. He would wear Pippa down eventually, would convince her that it was best for their child for them to be married. Except she wouldn't take his calls. When he showed up at Carrie's door, Pip refused to see him. He was about ready to kick that door in. It had been close to a month. He'd done as she asked for the first week. Then he called her. Daily. After two weeks, he tried to see her. Often. Luckily, Carrie was on his side and kept him informed. It didn't make him happy that Pippa was miserable too.

He was halfway home from the latest failed attempt to see her when his phone rang. Thinking it was Pippa and that she'd relented, he hit the Bluetooth button and answered. "Hey, ladybug."

"Excuse me?"

Kade recognized that voice. David Duncan. "Sorry, Mr. Duncan, I'm driving and was expecting a call from your daughter so I didn't check caller ID."

His finger hovered over the disconnect button but he decided to find out why Pippa's father would call him.

"If you want what is best for Pippa, stay away from her. While she might not be our biological daughter, she does carry the Duncan name. Millicent and I refuse to allow her to sully it."

"Sully your name? How is she doing that?"

"An illegitimate child is nothing to be proud of. But you wouldn't understand that."

Kade's fingers squeezed the steering wheel like he wanted to strangle Pippa's father. Approaching an exit, he veered over and took it. Pulling into a gas station, he slammed the transmission into Park and leashed his temper as Mr. Duncan continued.

"We're hoping Pippa comes to her senses. If she won't terminate the pregnancy, I'll arrange a private adoption and she can resume her life. Thankfully, she is keeping a low profile and has put plans for her idiotic foundation on hold."

In a frigid but calm voice, Kade said, "If Pippa decides she doesn't want our baby, custody comes to me."

"Yes, well. That is the problem, isn't it? You don't quite fit into our world, now, do you? It would be best if you stop attempting to contact Pippa. In fact, I will file a restraining order against you if you don't desist. You are not a suitable match. You never will be. Stay out of our lives, Waite. I won't warn you again." Pippa's father hung up without waiting for a response.

Kade's fiery temper was replaced by icy resolve. Duncan had implied that he was calling on Pippa's behalf. Was it true that she would deny him access to their child? Kade was not his father. He would not ignore—

His father. Cyrus Barron. Kade was a Barron. Is that what it would take to win Pippa over? He had one more ace up his sleeve before he went down that road. Actually, he had five of them. He dialed a number.

"Savannah? I have a favor to ask."

Pippa was not a happy camper as Carrie exited the highway headed toward the Crown B. Then she saw all the cars parked at the truck stop, and the people lined up to board a shuttle bus. As they neared the ranch, more cars lined the road and the drive when they pulled in. There was a carnival feel to the place—families everywhere. She recognized a passenger van from a local veteran's group, and one from Children's Hospital.

At the big house, the Barron brothers and their wives were holding court over a host of activities. Pony and horse rides. A tractor pulling a trailer piled high with hay and filled with laughing people. Dusty, the ranch dog, and Harley, the Newfoundland belonging to Cash and his new wife, Roxanne, pranced around wearing Camp Courage T-shirts.

Pippa's gaze found the tall dark-haired man holding a small boy on the saddle in front of him, riding around a small temporary corral. Dr. and Mrs. Amadi leaned on the railing waving. The boy offered a tentative smile in return.

What in the world was going on? She glared at Carrie. "Explain!"

Her best friend grinned. "Kade. He knew you wanted to do another fund-raiser so he put this together. With a little help. Deacon Tate is going to sing this afternoon. His whole band is coming. How awesome is this, Pip?"

She had to blink away the moisture in her eyes. "Kade did all this? For me?"

"Well, d'uh, darlin'. Who else would he do this for?"

Pippa stumbled out of Carrie's car and rushed to the corral. She only had eyes for Kade. He stopped his horse, dismounted and carefully lifted the child down. "Here you go, Tyler."

The boy stared up at the tall cowboy with shining eyes. "Thank you."

The whispered words were almost lost to the wind but Pip heard them, as did the Amadis. Mrs. Amadi grabbed Pip in a fierce hug. "He hasn't spoken in six months. Whatever you need, Pippa. We'll underwrite it."

She all but stumbled when the other woman suddenly released her and turned back to the boy crawling through the bars of the fence panel. Before Pippa could say anything to Kade, she was surrounded by a horde of other people. They led her away, all jabbering at her about this and that. She glanced back. Kade raised his hand to the brim of his cowboy hat and tipped it. How could she stay mad at a man who would do all this for her? How could she block him out of her life?

A young man leaning heavily on a cane, his gait uneven due to a prosthetic leg, approached her. "Somebody said you're the lady in charge?" His voice was soft, almost reverent, as he addressed her.

"In charge?" Her brain still hadn't quite caught up with events.

"Yes'm. Camp Courage?" She nodded and he continued. "My buddies—" He waved toward a group of men with various injuries. "We just want to say thank you. Getting outside, working…it makes us feel…" He ducked his head staring at the ground. "Whole." When he looked up, his smile was so shy, Pippa couldn't help herself. She hugged him, blinking back tears.

This! Camp Courage was all about this man and his friends and the children and everyone who'd been broken by life. "You're welcome."

More people came forward to thank her and when Deacon Tate and the Sons of Nashville started singing, she found herself sitting on a hay bale between the wounded warrior and Tyler Amadi. The little boy slipped his hand into hers and she fought back tears.

Later, as the sun slipped toward the Western hills, after the concert and with the crowd thinning, Pippa looked up from saying goodbye to another group to find Kade walking toward her leading a horse. "Want a ride, little girl?"

She bit down on her lips in a vain effort to hide her smile. "You are a very hard man to ignore."

"Yup."

Pippa spread her arms and turned in a slow circle. "Why did you do this?"

Kade stared at her, forehead furrowed in confusion. "Because it was important to you."

The internal box where she'd kept her emotions locked up burst like it had been hiding fireworks. She was pretty sure she loved this man. And whether he could say the words to her or not didn't seem all that important at the moment. His actions spoke so much louder.

"C'mon. I want to go for a ride."

Before she could react, Kade had lifted her into the saddle. He swung up behind her a moment later and reined the horse away from the lingering crowd. He settled her a little more comfortably across his thighs, one hand resting on her now-rounded tummy. She relaxed back against him, lulled by his touch and the horse's plodding gait.

"Thank you."

He kissed the back of her neck. "For what?"

"For doing all of this. For being you. For giving me the space I need."

"Will you marry me, Pippa?"

She rolled her eyes and swiveled her head around so she could kiss him. "No." Kade stiffened but she kissed him again. "I'm not ready. Not yet." Pippa could toss him that bone.

"I'm going to keep asking."

"I know. Maybe I'll surprise us both one of these days and say yes."

Fifteen

Kade was starting to hate the view from this window. He glared at his reflection in the glass. The door opened and he heard muffled voices. Shoes shuffled softly across the thick carpet. Refreshments had arrived. The waiting was wearing thin.

If he'd thought this out, he would have called Chance to set up an appointment. Instead, when he saw his baby at Pippa's ultrasound that morning, he'd made a snap decision after she declined his proposal yet again. At least they were in agreement about her father and his threats. Pippa had words with him and he hadn't contacted Kade again.

Upon his arrival in the Barron & Associates offices, he'd been ushered into Chance's inner sanctum. Kade had commenced with trying to explain his reason for being there in halting sentences, but Chance stopped him.

"I want to call a family meeting."

Now Kade was second-guessing everything. Cord and Cash arrived simultaneously and both greeted him from across the room. He nodded in silent response then returned his gaze to the vista beyond the window. He breathed through a momentary bout of panic when Clay appeared. He hadn't realized the senator was in town. About ten minutes later, Chase rushed in.

"Sorry. I had to convince Savannah to stay put." He tossed a lopsided grin Kade's direction. "She's really upset with you, dude. She wanted to be here."

Kade couldn't understand why she would, so he asked, "Why?"

Chase finished pouring a cup of coffee and grabbed a doughnut before answering. "For one thing, she's guessed what's going on and wants to officially be your sister. Well…sister-in-law. And you're avoiding her. She was really insistent about coming, though I'm not sure if it was because she wants to chew you out or defend you from us evil Barrons." He said the last with a mischievous grin but quickly sobered. "So…seriously, bro. She's feeling hurt. Why *are* you avoiding her?"

Kade dropped his chin to his chest and stared at the toes of his boots. He didn't want to answer that question—not in front of these men, one of whom was Savannah's husband. Even though Chase and Savannah were polar opposites, they loved each other deeply and Kade was happy for her. Chase continued staring at him, waiting for his answer.

"Yeah, about that. Been sorta busy. I'll call her."

"When?" Kade glanced up to discover amused annoyance on Chase's face. "Because she's gonna want to know. Look, bro. We've been really patient and we—" he swept a hand across the room to encompass his brothers "—have done our best to keep the wives out of the loop. You have no idea what they're like. Well, Savannah maybe, but I'm tellin' ya, we are all under pressure." Chase's grin was unrepentant. "Chance insisted we give you space, especially after that bombshell you dropped about dating Pippa. You have met our wives, right? Trying to hold them back is like trying to stop a flash flood with a bucket of sand."

Chance fixed a withering stare on his younger brother. "Cool it, Chase."

Kade knew Chase was teasing and it made him feel odd. He'd always maintained a friendly aloofness in his dealings with the Barron brothers. With Cyrus Barron, the relationship had most definitely been employer and employee.

When Chance appeared next to him, he concentrated on keeping his emotions in check.

"It doesn't have to be this hard, Kade."

"Did you know?" He studied Chance, then shifted his gaze to the other men seated around the conference table. "Did you know who I am?"

"Not for sure," Chance replied. "We suspected you were related to us, but the old man never let on you were anything more than his ranch manager. That said, when the will named you, we weren't exactly shocked either."

Jamming his hands into his front pockets so Chance

wouldn't see the fists he made, Kade turned his head just enough to see his half brother in profile. "It doesn't make you mad? Any of you? I'm...nobody, and your father decreed that y'all had to hand over a major part of your inheritance to me. How does that not make you angry?"

Chance leaned his shoulder against the window. After a long moment of studying Kade, he spoke. "He was your father, too, Kade. That makes you our brother, whether you accept us or not. Does this situation suck? Absolutely." Chance quickly held up his hand to stay the argument forming on Kade's lips. "We already have what we want from this deal. That's not why I say it sucks. We know you. We understand that the ranch means everything to you. Nothing has been done yet. I filed an injunction against the ranch trustees to give you time to decide."

Glancing around at his brothers, Chance returned his focus to Kade. "If it was up to us, you wouldn't have to do a thing to keep your job. And I want to apologize to you. It never occurred to me that the old man would so totally screw things up. The ranch has always been like home to us, but I think that has more to do with the fact that Big John and Miz Beth live there. Even so, I knew what an SOB Cyrus could be. When I originally set up the family trust that secured what was important to each of us—knowing he would mess with things to get his way—I just didn't believe that our father would be this callous."

Chance inhaled and raised his chin, as if avoiding a blow. "If I had, I would have taken steps to prevent it.

The old man outfoxed us. He outmaneuvered me and set up a blind trust that I can't break. Believe me, after seeing your reaction when Stephenson read the will, I looked into it. I'm sorry."

"We're all to blame, Chance," Clay said, walking over. "Each of us had our own little fiefdom picked out. Our father loved to play us against each other, even when we were kids." He tilted his head toward Chase and Cash. "Especially after you two came along." He offered a wry grin to the twins. "Cord, Chance and I didn't buy into his BS. And Kade, we still don't. When he first hired you, I remembered wondering from the moment I saw you. The more we were around you, the more we wondered. But like Chance said, the old man never gave a hint. It's up to you whether you want to change your name." Clay gripped Kade's shoulder. "We'd be proud to call you brother whether your last name is Waite or Barron."

Kade stared at the one brother who'd remained silent. Cash returned his gaze without a flinch. "How do you feel about this?" Kade asked.

Cash continued to watch him and the silence stretched thin—almost to the breaking point—before he spoke. "I did a background check on you when I took over Barron Security."

He wasn't surprised but he waited, figuring Cash had more to say. He wasn't disappointed.

"There was no paper trail, no indication whatsoever that you were one of us. Trust me when I say that the old man, all of us, in fact, have dealt with our share of gold diggers who wanted a piece of our pie. Then there was you. You graduated from OSU with a degree in agricultural science. You came to work here. Dad was adamant about hiring you. I remember him and the head wrangler arguing about it. Manuel was convinced you were too young and inexperienced. Not that he wanted to take on the place. None of us did. Dad stuck Cord in charge—nominally—as CEO of Barron Land and Cattle."

Pausing to sip from his coffee cup, Cash looked at each of his brothers before his gaze settled once more on Kade. "I didn't trust you. I watched, double-checked the books, had my forensic accountant stay on top of things."

Kade stiffened at this admission. This was what he'd been expecting all along—that proverbial other shoe. He knew there was no way it could be all flowers and sunshine with the brothers.

"Imagine my surprise," Cash continued, "when you proved me wrong. Everything you did, you did for the Crown B. The grazing program you initiated. The breeding program where you emphasized quality over quantity. Because of that, you demanded and got top dollar on our stocker calves. And the horses?" He looked to Chance. "That's your area of expertise, Chance. Your assessment?"

Chance barked out a short laugh. "You tryin' to get me in trouble, little brother? The whole reason I met Cassidy was because the old man wanted to get his hands on her quarter horse stud." He cut his eyes to Kade. "Was it you who wanted Doc?"

"Not exactly. I wanted a stud *like* Doc but I thought I could breed him on my own."

Chance nudged Kade's shoulder with his own. "I figured it was the old man's grudge against Cassie's dad. And you were right. You did breed a super horse. Imp is…" He laughed again, humor suffusing the sound. "Amazing. And my wife is totally jealous."

That startled a chuckle out of Kade. "She has a yearling mare I'm keeping my eye on—"

"And that sums it up," Cash interrupted. "Kade, you're like one of those old Louis L'Amour cowboys." He addressed his brothers with his next comment. "Y'all remember all those paperbacks up in the playroom at the ranch? Granddad was always reading them. L'Amour and Zane Grey. One of the main themes in those books was riding for the brand. You do, Kade. You've always done what was right for the Crown B. Not for yourself, but because it was best for the ranch and therefore the family. In fact, you're such a white hat, it's kinda scary."

"Bottom line," Clay said. "You're our brother. To us, your decision should be easy. The ranch would be yours. What's to even think about? But we aren't you. We grew up Barrons. You grew up…not." He winced a little. "Sorry. For a man used to making speeches, that was lame. I need Georgie here. My wife knows exactly what to say. Thankfully, she still writes my speeches." He chuckled, then his expression turned serious. "Thing is, we can't force you to choose one way or the other. But we also can't fix the situation about your job if you don't accept us as family. Our father tied our hands with the trustees he appointed."

We can't force you to accept us as family. That's not precisely what Clay said, but that's what Kade heard. Did he have a choice in this? If he walked away, his unborn child would suffer. If he stayed, he lost who he was. But was that the truth? He didn't want to consider that Pippa might be correct—that names didn't matter when it came down to what made a person. Still, he knew *who* Kaden Waite was. He had no clue about Kaden Barron. If he signed the papers, what would happen when he woke up the day after? Would he recognize the face staring back from the mirror?

Kade mentally shook himself. That was a ludicrous reaction and he knew it. He could walk out of this room. He could find another job on another ranch. But. And that *but* was what kept him standing here. Pippa was having his child. She refused to marry him, and he needed to stay close. He hoped to persuade her because the idea of his child growing up without his father's name—and more importantly—without his father? The whole notion was unthinkable. They fought over this constantly and each time, his heart shredded a little more. Why couldn't she understand his need to provide for her and the baby, and to ensure the baby had his name? Whichever name he chose. He almost laughed at the irony. Here he was insisting their baby carry his name and he didn't even know what it was… or would be.

Without conscious thought, he placed his palm on the back of his neck and rubbed at the tension lodged there. Kade was thankful he'd skipped breakfast. His stomach ached as if he'd eaten bad food and a wave of nausea rolled over him. This shouldn't be such a big deal, but it was. He studied each of his new brothers, considered what he knew of them.

Clay was the oldest. He'd been running for Congress when Kade first went to work at the Crown B. He'd found the older man to be intense, focused and honorable. He'd also been aloof and mostly blind to Cyrus Barron's machinations. Until he'd fallen in love with the woman who'd become his wife. Clay had walked away from his campaign for the presidency because Georgie became ill and needed him. Kade had been surprised.

Of all the Barrons, the next brother in line would most likely identify with Kade's dilemma. Cord had reunited with his first love after discovering she'd had his son—and had hidden the fact. At least Pippa wasn't trying that. Kade would go freaking crazy if she tried. Now Cord, Jolie and CJ were a family.

The youngest of the first set of Barron brothers, Chance had been the first to break away from their father's yoke. He'd stood up to Cyrus—and his brothers—in order to marry the woman who'd roped his heart. Now Chance and Cassidy were building a ranch and breeding program that might rival the Crown B's one day.

That left the twins, born to Cyrus' second wife. For all that Chase and Cash were identical in looks, their personalities were almost exact opposites. Chase was the carefree playboy living the high life in Vegas, Hollywood and Nashville. He'd been roped and tied by a real Oklahoma cowgirl. Kade still hadn't quite wrapped his brain around that development nor completely reconciled the fact that the girl he considered his kid sister had married and fallen in love with Chase—in that order.

Cash was the black sheep of the family, only that wasn't totally fair. From what Kade had observed, the youngest Barron was the one most entrenched—or maybe ensnared was the better description—in the Barron patriarch's schemes. In the end, though, Cash had seen the light. His brothers kept him in the fold and Cash's new wife had brought him lightness and laughter.

Kade had never been one to speak ill of the dead but looking around the table at the five Barron brothers, they were in a much better place now their father was gone. Kade had always been a student of human nature and none of the Barrons appeared to be lying when they spoke of the ranch and the fact it should be his. All they asked was that it remain their home as well. As if he would really toss Big John and Miz Beth out? He didn't want the big house. It wasn't his home. The manager's house? He'd made the place his and it had a second, smaller bedroom that would work as a nursery.

Since his grandfather's death, Kade hadn't been back to Davis much. His grandmother no longer recognized him and his mother had started a life without him once he left for college. He hadn't liked the reason she kept his parentage from him. These five men and their wives were waiting to welcome him into their family as a full-fledged member. A brother.

Turning away to stare out the window again, Kade considered his options. In the end, the reality of this decision came down to his responsibilities.

"Where do I sign?"

Sixteen

Kade signed slowly, each letter almost painful to put to paper. He wondered how long it would take him to feel comfortable writing his new name. He almost smiled thinking maybe he should practice like the girls in high school used to do, filling up pages of lined notebook paper writing their "married" names whenever they dated a boy more than a couple of times.

Kaden William Waite. Kaden William Barron. His hand was steady, which surprised him a bit. He didn't want to think about this, what he was doing. He didn't want to be angry about getting shoved in this corner. He'd searched for a way out of the conundrum and hadn't found one. All the conversations echoed in his head.

He'd originally told Pippa, "I can't be a Waite. I have to be a Barron."

Her reply had basically been *So what*? and that made him angry. Her exact words were, *Is that so bad*? She went on to explain her thought process, telling him he would be the same man, not someone different. *You'd still be Kaden. The name doesn't make a person. It's just a label.*

But names and labels defined a person, didn't they? He thought back to the beginning when he first found out. Each of the Barrons—his brothers—had reached out to him. They hadn't written him off, hadn't pushed things. Chance's reaction had been measured. Since he was an attorney, it made sense. He understood the shock, and Chance wanted to talk things out, discuss the situation.

Clay, as the oldest brother, had taken a more pragmatic approach—a simple welcome to the family and a suggestion to talk to Chance. Cord, next oldest, had been blunt. To Cord, walking away was a stupid reaction, but he expressed a willingness to wait for Kade to come to terms. *We're here when you're ready*, he'd said. Cash and Chase had double-teamed him as twins would. Cash had been teasing—talking about hunting Kade down, then offering to meet for a beer and conversation. Chase had mentioned their wives. Since Chance's marriage to Cassie, Kade had seen just how the women worked. And everything they did was for the good of their men.

His chest burned at that thought. He could admit he was jealous of his brothers now. Calling them that still felt strange but it got easier each time. All he had to do was look at them with their wives to know how much love was there. He *wanted* that. And he wanted it with Pippa. Maybe as a Barron, she would find his name suitable for their child.

Names were important, no matter what others said to him. Cyrus Barron thought bestowing his name on his bastard son was so important that he came back from the grave to force the name on Kade.

His mother's voice whispered in his ear. *That's a terrible position to be in, but have you considered this?* He remembered the expression on her face as she'd asked that question—the sadness mixed with concern. *What if I'd given you up?* He could have been in the same position as Pippa. He would have been adopted. And he definitely wouldn't be Kaden Waite. Or Kaden Barron.

Rose had barely given him time to digest that when she'd hit him with her next hypothetical question. *What if he'd been single and we'd married?* In the time since his talk with her, he had contemplated that one. A lot. He wasn't a physicist and the whole idea of parallel dimensions was a little beyond him, but if that had happened, the odds of Chase and Cash being born were probably between slim and none. It was more than he could—or wanted to—wrap his head around.

He hesitated over writing his last name. His mom's last question was the one that he considered now. *What if I'd simply added his name to your birth certificate?* When he looked down at the papers on the conference table in front of him, he saw the answer she'd given him. Kaden William Barron.

"So what happens now?"

Chance's expression was solemn. "I've already

made arrangements with Judge Nelligan. We're doing the name change under an emergency order. The judge has waived the publication period and is signing under seal so the news won't be common knowledge until we're ready to go public. He's expecting us as soon as we can walk over."

Once the gears were set in motion, everything happened with lightning-speed. When Kade walked from Barron Tower to the Oklahoma County Courthouse, all five Barrons were with him. It felt strange. In a few minutes, there would be six Barron brothers. They cleared security then shouldered their way through the crowd getting off an elevator. Kade was very conscious of the looks they received, looks the others seemed oblivious to. He wondered if he'd ever get to a point when he wouldn't notice.

The elevator dinged for the third floor and Chance got off first, the other Barrons following. They passed groups of people and Kade noticed a woman watching the six of them. She looked vaguely familiar but he couldn't place where he might know her from.

When his party stopped in front of the judge's chamber, he glanced back at her. She had her smartphone out and pointed down the hallway toward them. He quickly turned his back.

The judge's chamber was comprised of a waiting room and the judge's office, along with offices for his bailiff and clerk. Kade and Chance entered the inner office, leaving the rest of their brothers in the outer area. Judge Nelligan rose to shake hands with Chance, who introduced Kade.

"I've got the court clerk coming up here with his seal. We'll get this taken care of as soon as he gets here." A quick tap on the door heralded the clerk's arrival.

Kade wasn't sure what he expected to happen. Chance hadn't prepared him and he was glad there wasn't any sort of real ceremony—just more signatures under the watchful eye of the court clerk, who then stamped the legal papers. Just like that, he was Kaden Barron.

His brothers stood as he and Chance exited. Kade expected handshakes. He got hugs.

"Welcome to the family, Kade."

"About freaking time."

"Y'all realize there's an even number now."

Deep voices rimmed with laughter and affection surrounded him. He should have felt overwhelmed. He didn't. He felt…accepted. And the emotion left him reeling. He just hoped he'd have time to get his bearings before his world changed even more.

Furious beyond all reason, Pippa drove straight to the ranch. This was not a conversation to hold over the phone. She flew past the big house and skidded to a stop in front of the ranch office. Storming inside, she glared at the woman occupying the front desk.

"Where is he, Selena?"

The ranch secretary shrugged. "Haven't seen him this morning."

A moment later, Pippa had both hands on the desk and was leaning forward to glower at the woman. "Don't cover for him."

"I'm not, Pippa. I really haven't seen him. He could be

at his house, one of the barns or he could be out on the ranch somewhere. He doesn't always check in with me."

"He's not answering his phone."

That made Selena laugh. "Well, d'uh. All things considered, would you?"

And that was the problem, wasn't it? Her phone had blown up with calls and text messages as soon as the news leaked, along with a cell phone video. "If he comes back, you tell him to keep his butt right here until I've talked to him."

Selena arched a brow and, fighting a grin, snapped a salute. "Yes, ma'am."

Pippa retreated from the office and stood on the porch wondering what to do. A musical whistle made up her mind. She knew that sound—Kade calling Imp. With determination in every step, she headed to the large corral adjacent the horse barn. She stopped as she turned the corner and saw Kade.

His forearms rested on the top rail of the fence. His stance was relaxed, feet shoulder-width apart. Worn jeans fit him in all the right places and the white T-shirt stretched across his broad torso and muscular biceps. He wore a baseball cap, the bill tipped up as he watched Imp, his pride and joy, frolic with two other yearling colts.

"Why didn't you answer your phone?" she demanded as she stomped toward him.

He turned his head slightly to acknowledge her presence before he returned his attention to the corral.

"Well?" she asked again as she reached him.

"I left my phone at the house."

Pippa huffed. "Likely excuse."

That got an angry glance from Kade. "I'm not glued to the thing like most people."

"What's that supposed to mean?"

"Nothing, Pippa. Nothing at all." He sounded worn out but she was too wound up to really notice.

"How could you!" she challenged.

He ignored her.

"Seriously, Kade. This is…it's…not a little thing."

"No. Not by a long shot." His jaw worked as though he was gritting his teeth.

"That's an understatement because I was trying to be nice. This is…it's huge. You've just changed everything. You should have asked me." Pippa was all but quivering from pent-up anger. "This affects me too. And the baby."

Kade gripped the top rail of the fence until his knuckles turned white. "I'm aware of that."

She wanted to hit him, to pound her fists against his chest. She felt hot and cold all at the same time. "Why? Why would you do this without telling me?" Both hands lifted, fists closed, and she fought her urges. "Do you have any idea how I felt waking up to the news? Carrie came running in screaming, and bounced on my bed. She was thrilled beyond reason."

He continued staring into the corral, watching the three horses mill around. "Do you have any idea how I felt signing the papers?" His voice was a rough whisper, barely more than the sound of sandpaper on wood.

"I don't care!" Pippa snapped at him as she jerked her phone out of her pocket and waved it in front of him. "It's already started. My mother. My father. Everyone involved. You've let them win because you are *acceptable* now. You're a freaking Barron. The prodigal son. The lost heir. She's hiring a wedding planner this morning."

He looked at her then and what she saw on his face made her take a step back. "Did you tell her that's a waste of time because you refuse to marry me?"

"I won't marry you just to keep my child from being a bastard."

"It's my child too."

"Not if I have anything to say about it."

Pippa didn't think Kade could appear any more intimidating than when she'd first walked up but looking at him now? His face had turned to chiseled granite and his eyes looked as hard as agate.

"Be very careful what you say next, Pippa."

She didn't speak. She reacted, her hand flying out to slap him. The sound was so sharp it sent the horses galloping to the other side of the corral. Kade didn't move but his face went completely blank; all the life fled from his eyes. Bile rose in Pippa's throat, threatening to choke her, but she'd gone too far to turn back now.

"We're done." She turned on her heel, and barely managing to keep her head and shoulders straight, she walked with great deliberation back the way she'd come. As she turned the corner of the barn, she glanced back. Kade hadn't moved.

Kade stared into the amber liquid in the beer mug. He'd come to Shorty's to get drunk, not share his feelings with his…brothers. The word froze his brain.

Cash occupied the stool on his left while Cord leaned

against the bar on his right. They bracketed him and he fought a wave of claustrophobia.

"How did you find me?"

Cash laughed heartily and slapped him on the back. "You forget what I do for a living, Kade."

"Selena called you."

"No," Cord said. "She called Chance. She saw Pippa's Highlander tearing down the drive and then your truck doing the same a few minutes later."

"And Chance called me. I pinged your cell phone. Then I called Cord."

Kade slowly glanced from one man to the other. "You pinged my phone? How does that work?"

Smirking, Cash said, "If I revealed my methods, I'd have to kill you. Or something." After a dry chuckle, he added, "That was a joke, dude. You're supposed to laugh."

"Not much to laugh about just now," Kade admitted.

Cord took several deep swallows of his beer. "You gonna explain?"

"She's pissed."

"What did you do?"

Killing his beer in one long drink, Kade snarled, "I signed the damn papers."

"Why is she mad about that?" Cash exchanged a look with Cord.

"I didn't tell her I was changing my name."

The brothers exchanged a second look. Kade, staring in the mirror behind the bar, missed nothing. It was Cord's turn to question him. "So…why is that a problem? All things considered, I'd think she'd be thrilled."

Kade didn't respond, defaulting to killing the beer in his mug with long gulps. Silence stretched between them until the jukebox came to life and the voice of Kenny Chesney crooned his song, "There Goes My Life." Kade stilled, listening to the words—the story of a boy and a girl and the baby they made, all set around a refrain that echoed the song's title. He was ready to change his life, to give up who he was so he could become who Pippa and their child needed. He couldn't understand why she was so obstinate. And why she was so mad about what he'd done. He'd done it for her. For their baby.

He didn't realize a tear had escaped until Cord gripped his shoulder. He angrily brushed his shirtsleeve across his cheek when he realized his skin was wet.

"Man, you need to talk to us," Cash encouraged. "There's obviously something more going on here."

"She's pregnant."

Seventeen

Was she being foolish? After her parents' declaration, Pippa had decided to search for her birth family. This was probably a stupid idea, considering how messed up everything was between her and Kade. Still, she needed to find out, needed to know where she came from. Odd how her life now paralleled Kade's. She thought they were moving toward something truly special. Then he'd done the unthinkable and she'd confronted him. Could she fault him for accepting his birth family when she was so desperately searching for her own? Maybe once she knew about her roots she'd understand. Maybe then she would call him and they could talk.

When she first decided to do this, Pippa had gone straight to Chance to get him to file for her original birth certificate. When he'd handed it to her, she'd stared at it—at her birth name and the name of her birth mother. Disappointment had washed over her when no father was listed and for a moment, she understood how Kade might feel, given his situation. Still, she had her original name. Marcia Rae Gore. She'd tasted it on the tip of her tongue like it was a rare vintage of wine as she'd read it the first time. After adjusting to the idea of being adopted and having been born with another name, she'd gone hunting.

When she found no leads, she'd turned the search over to a professional—Cash Barron. Thirty-two days later, Cash had called and asked for a meeting at his office. Now she was here, sitting across from him at his desk. A large envelope sat on the blotter in front of him.

"Did you find anything?" She hated that her voice quavered. This shouldn't have been so nerve-racking.

Cash watched her for a tense moment. "Are you sure you want to do this?"

Pippa stared at the envelope resting on the desk. Her heart pounded and she kept her hands clutched in her lap so Cash wouldn't see how badly they were trembling. Taking deep breaths to ease her nerves, she eventually nodded.

He held out the envelope without a word though the expression on his face spoke volumes. She reached for it but had to shake the numbness out of her hand before accepting.

Pushing back from his desk, Cash said, "I'll give you some privacy."

"No!" Her demand came out far more forcefully than

she'd anticipated. "No," she added in a quieter tone. "Is it bad? I...the way you're acting. It's bad news, isn't it?"

Cash scrutinized her, his expression not giving anything away. "I don't know how to answer that question, Pippa." He drummed the desk with the fingers of his right hand but then stilled as he continued. "I believe Kade should be here when you open it."

Shocked, her mouth dropped open. "Kade? Why on earth would you even think of him?"

Cash's gaze dropped pointedly to her midsection where she'd begun to show more than a baby bump. "Because he has an investment in this too. And..." Cash's voice softened. "Because he cares about you, about your baby."

"Oh, he's all about the baby," she snapped. "He's all about having his name on the birth certificate."

Arching a brow, Cash didn't say anything. When she didn't continue, he spoke. "It's more than that, Pippa, and I think you know it."

"You don't know anything about it, Cash. About us. Kade and me. He's all *Let's get married because my baby needs a father*. That's stupid. We don't have to get married. In fact, I don't want to get married." She glared when Cash snorted in disbelief. "I don't. Kade doesn't love me. Why would I marry someone who is only doing it out of some misguided sense of obligation? What kind of home is that for a baby? Just stay out of it. You aren't involved."

"Kade is my brother, Pip. And that baby will be my niece or nephew. We're all involved."

"Really? You're all about family now, Cash? Heck,

you didn't know anything about him being family until a few months ago."

He inhaled as if reaching for patience. When he continued, he used a soft voice and spoke carefully. "I know what's in the envelope, hon. Please, let me call Kade."

Her stomach knotted up and she had to breathe around the clutch in her chest. She'd started this search to find answers to her medical history. She had a deep-seated fear there would be some horrible genetic anomaly or medical issue in her biological family. Cash had never been known for his empathy, but the compassionate look on his face at this moment terrified her. "It's bad. Really bad, isn't it?"

Cash didn't say a word; he just reached for the phone on his desk.

When the phone on Chance's desk beeped, he held up a finger for Kade to wait. Figuring it was business important enough for Chance's assistant to interrupt their meeting, Kade rose and walked to the bookshelf across the office. He expected it to be filled with law books. He was surprised to discover biographies, histories and a whole shelf dedicated to classic science fiction and Westerns. He turned to discover Chance still on the phone but watching him intently.

"No, this can wait. We'll be right down." Chance hung up and stood. "That was Cash. Pippa is in his office. We need to get down there."

Kade couldn't move. Couldn't breathe. Couldn't talk. He could barely put one foot in front of the other for all the thoughts winging through his brain. Why was she with Cash? Was she hurt? What had happened? He blinked, realized Chance was already to the door of the office. He followed hot on the other man's heels as they rushed toward the interior stairwell. Cash's office was located only two floors down. He and Chance could cover the distance faster on the stairs than waiting for the elevator.

No one stopped them as they slammed through the massive doors of Barron Security and headed toward Cash's private office. Cheri, Cash's assistant, waved them toward his door. Chance tapped twice, then opened it. He stepped back to let Kade precede him into the room. Kade stopped when he saw Pippa, looking frightened and lost, sitting in one of the armchairs.

His first instinct was to rush to her and pull her into a hug. His second was to throw a punch at Cash since the other man obviously had something to do with putting that look on Pippa's face. It was, however, his third— and most measured—instinct that prevailed, especially as Pippa's expression clouded over with anger when she realized he was in the room.

Cash stood up behind his desk. "Thanks for coming, Kade. I suspect Pippa will need you once she reads what's in that envelope. Chance and I will be outside if you two need us."

With that, Cash and Chance exited the office, leaving him alone with Pippa. She was holding a large envelope. He approached her slowly, hands loose at his sides, like he would with a skittish horse. He checked her over. Her stomach had rounded even more than the last time he'd seen her, but she looked tired and the dark circles under her eyes concerned him. "Pippa?"

"Go away, Kade."

Her shoulders slumped and she sounded worn out. He hadn't seen her in more than a month. He had no clue why she was sitting here in Cash's office, but he was starting to wonder if Cash and Chance had set him up. He wouldn't put it past them—or any of the Barrons, their wives included. The whole family seemed intent on getting him hooked up with Pippa.

Kade squatted down on his heels next to her chair, his hand on the wooden arm, ostensibly to maintain his balance. "What's going on, ladybug?"

"None of your business, Kade."

"It is if it's something that concerns you."

She shifted away from him but it appeared to be more so she could twist to look at him than to put distance between them. "Do you really not know?"

"Not a clue. I was up in Chance's office going over some paperwork regarding the transfer of the Crown B. The next thing I know, he's on the phone. He hangs up, tells me we need to get down here and…" He spread his hands. "Here I am."

Pippa huffed out a breath and started to push a lock of her hair back when she seemed to realize she was still holding the envelope. Kade hooked the errant strand with his finger and tucked it behind her ear. "Talk to me, Pip. Please?"

"The fight I had with my parents. It started because I wanted a medical history. That's when Moth… Millicent told me I was adopted. It might be dumb, or insignificant in the long run, but I want to know where I came from. What and who I am. What health problems I might have or could pass on. So, after thinking about it, I hired Chance. He petitioned to get my birth certificate. The original one. And my adoption papers."

Kade did his best not to tense. This was the first he'd heard of her request. "Is that what's in the envelope?"

"No. I got those about two months ago. My birth name was Marcia Rae Gore. My mother was listed but not my father."

He winced. Yeah, he knew all about that kind of birth certificate. He jerked when her hand landed on his arm. He immediately schooled his expression.

"I'm sorry, Kade. I wasn't thinking. I…it's weird. I was disappointed that I didn't have a name to put with my father, but I had my mother's. It was enough." She lifted one shoulder in a delicate shrug. "Or I thought it would be. Since I had her name, I figured it would be easy enough to locate her."

"Did you?"

Pippa shook her head. "No. I thought I had decent computer search skills and Carrie's mother is into genealogy. We couldn't find anything." She looked away and inhaled. "I asked Cash to do a search for her. I mean, that's what he does, right?"

Her gaze flicked to him then, as if asking his…his what? Permission? Acceptance? This was the longest conversation they'd had since she stormed out of the barn. He didn't want to break this fragile truce springing up between them. "Yeah, it's one of the things he does. Background checks, searching for missing persons. Stuff like that. You were smart to come to him."

"You think so?"

The hope on her face almost broke his heart. Cash knew he and Pippa were estranged. For him to arrange for Kade's presence—and there was no doubt in his mind that this was anything *but* a setup—meant that whatever was in that envelope was going to upset Pippa.

"Yeah, he's the best. I'm guessing he found something?"

Glancing at the envelope, she nodded. "Yeah. But I haven't opened it yet." She suddenly thrust it at him. "Will you open it?"

He didn't immediately take the envelope. Instead, he stared into her eyes. He was praying this was a break in their stalemate, that she was giving him an opening so he could come back into her life. But he had to be positive this was the case. "Are you sure you want *me* to do that?"

Pippa stared back, her expression as solemn as his own surely was. She didn't speak for a long moment. Then she pressed her lips together and nodded—a short, jerky motion. "Yes. Please?"

He accepted the envelope. It hadn't been sealed so he slid out the small sheaf of papers inside.

"Read it, Kade. Then tell me what it says." Pippa sounded certain even as her voice quavered slightly.

"Okay." He partially rose and pulled the second guest chair closer so he could sit right next to her. Settling into the padded leather, he scanned the first page. Then the second. By the third, he had to fight to keep any emotion off his face. He had no idea how Pippa would react to this news. He suspected she wouldn't take it well. He wouldn't if their places were reversed.

Just in case he'd misread the information, Kade started at the beginning, reading slowly this time through. Pippa's hand touched his thigh, squeezed gently. He dropped his hand to take hers, lacing their fingers. He finished the first page and, letting go of Pippa for a brief moment, placed it face down on Cash's desk. He took her hand again and continued reading, repeating his action with each page. He didn't stop until he'd read the last word.

He hadn't been mistaken on his first reading. And he knew Cash would have been extra thorough in this investigation. How was he going to tell her the messy details that were so neatly laid out in print? His chest hurt for Pippa, and he wasn't sure he could speak around the lump in his throat. Her hand trembled in his and he gave it a soft squeeze.

"It's really bad, isn't it?" Pippa shook her head. "No, don't say anything. When I asked Cash the same thing, he told me he didn't know what to say, and he called you to come."

"Yeah, he called me." Kade cut his gaze toward the door. "I'm glad I was close by, ladybug."

"I'm scared, Kade. You should just tell me. You know, like ripping off a bandage."

He wanted to gather her into his lap so he could cradle her. He didn't want to tell her what Cash had uncovered, not while looking into her scared eyes. He'd much prefer whispering it into her hair with the hopes she wouldn't hear. But he couldn't do any of those things.

While she might not realize what she was doing, he did. She trusted him enough to take the bad news and give it to her.

He swallowed, hard. The first word he tried to speak got caught and he had to clear his throat. "Your mother. She's still alive. And you have siblings. Two sisters and two brothers."

She squeezed his hand so hard, she all but cut off the blood flow. Kade did his best to ignore the tears swimming in her eyes.

"That's…it's wonderful, isn't it?"

She sounded so damned hopeful he didn't want to burst her bubble. So how did he answer that? "There's something else, Pippa." Kade inhaled. "There's a real possibility they aren't your half-siblings. You might share the same father."

Pippa stared at him, confusion infiltrating her once hopeful expression. "The same father?"

"Yeah, sweetheart. And that's not all." *Like ripping off a Band-Aid*, he thought. "Your oldest sister. Her name is Marcia Rae."

Eighteen

"Wait. What?" Pippa felt bruised as she jumped out of the chair and lunged for the neat stack of papers Kade had meticulously built on the front edge of Cash's desk. She had a sister with the same name? A *full* sister? She couldn't comprehend any of this.

"Easy, ladybug." Kade intercepted her hands and blocked her from knocking the papers to the floor. He circled her waist with a strong arm and eased her against him.

Pippa collapsed in his arms, forgetting her anger toward him for a moment. He was here. He was warm and strong, and in this moment, she realized he *did* care about her. It wasn't love, but he wasn't just some Neanderthal beating his chest about names.

"Come sit on the couch, sweetheart. I'll bring the papers and you can read them. Okay?"

She allowed herself to be guided to the leather sofa and sank into its buttery softness. Pippa looked up at Kade. She didn't know what to do and that bothered her. She'd never been indecisive, but at present, she was so stunned she couldn't decide anything. Kade cupped her cheek in his palm.

"I'll be right back, ladybug. I want to make sure it's okay for us to stay here for a while."

Oh. She'd forgotten for a moment that she was in Cash's office. He probably had business to attend to and she was in the way. She was embarrassed that she was falling apart. Wrapping her arms around herself to stop her trembling, she nodded. She was in no shape to leave, and she was honest enough to admit that fact.

Kade dropped a soft kiss on her forehead, then strode across the room and disappeared into the outer office. Her shivering grew more pronounced. She had a mother. Sisters. Brothers. She maybe had a father—an unexpected fact given her original birth certificate. But why would her mother give her sister the same name as her? Why would her mother give her away yet have four other children with the man who might have impregnated her the first time?

Was she defective in some way that her mother recognized but that didn't show? Could she be so damaged her mother didn't want to keep her? She buried her face in her hands. She wanted to cry. Needed to cry. But she couldn't. All the tears stayed locked inside her, as did the sobs threatening but never manifesting. Pippa lifted her head and forced it back in a futile attempt to ease the tenseness in her neck and shoulders. She opened her eyes. The papers still waiting on the edge of Cash's desk drew her gaze like a powerful magnet.

She needed to read the words for herself. She should just stand up. Walk over there. Sit in that chair. Read every word in that report. But she didn't move. Couldn't move. She felt drained of all energy. Her initial excitement had deflated, flatlined and been replaced by a sense of dread. Marcia Rae. Her birth name. She'd just learned that's who she was—had been, she mentally corrected. For how long? How old had she been before her parents adopted her? The fact that another girl had her name shouldn't matter. But it did. It mattered a lot. And it hurt, the knowledge ripping through her heart like a dull knife hacking at her emotions.

Where was Kade? She really needed him here. His strength, his calm, she needed those desperately. Had he left the office so he could get away from her? She wouldn't blame him. She was an emotional wreck. What man would want to put up with a hormonal pregnant woman whose world had just dissolved around her? And yes, she could also admit, she was acting the drama queen. All things considered, she had the right to her meltdown.

Kade didn't want to leave Pippa alone for very long. He did want to get her a cup of tea. She needed something… normal, something routine, comforting. If he couldn't hold her, he'd give her something hot to drink because he couldn't think of anything else to do.

He stepped through the door to find not only Cash and Chance, but Cord had joined them as well. Kade pulled up short. He didn't need this whole brother triple-team thing, nor did he have time for their games and pretense at family solidarity.

"Is she okay?" Cord asked in a quiet voice, glancing toward the closed door. That's when Kade realized the other two were on their cell phones. All three men wore concerned expressions.

"Stand by, Chase," Cash said, looking expectantly at Kade.

"He just came out, Clay. I'll find out and call you back." Chance thumbed off his phone.

"Why are you all here?" Kade winced inwardly. He hadn't meant for his tone to sound so accusatory and defensive. Okay, maybe he had, but he was belatedly realizing that the Barrons were truly concerned about Pippa and her situation—and by extension, himself. He closed his eyes and lowered his head. After a few breaths, he straightened and faced them. "Look, I'm sorry. That was uncalled for."

Cord, who was standing the nearest, gripped Kade's shoulder. "S'okay, man. You're worried about your lady. And I'm pretty certain you're still trying to wrap your head around the whole family thing."

"We're here because we care, Kade," Cash cut in. "We may fight like junkyard dogs amongst ourselves, but if you come at one of us, you come at all of us." He lifted his shoulders in an apologetic shrug and added in a rueful tone, "I had to figure that out for myself."

Chance nodded his agreement. "We always have each other's backs, but that doesn't stop us from calling each other out when we've screwed up."

Kade noticed both Cord and Chance were staring at Cash who continued to look sheepish. The three looked so much alike, their family relationship was apparent but it was the real affection they showed that rocked him.

"Look, I just came out to see if I could get Pippa a cup of tea or something." Kade jammed his thumbs in his front pockets. "I don't even know if she likes hot tea. I just..." His voice trailed off.

"You need to do something for her," Chance filled in. "We get that. We've all been there."

"Hot tea coming up." Cash was quick to volunteer. "And there's a blanket—an afghan or something—behind the pillows on the far end of the couch. Roxie gets cold sometimes. Just in case."

"Whatever you need, Kade, whatever Pippa needs, we're here for you." Cord's hand still rested on his shoulder, and his brother gave another squeeze to show support.

It was as though a lightbulb went off in Kade's head. No, not a lightbulb, something more subtle, not as bright but just as warm...and enlightening. Family. Brothers. Love given with no strings attached. It was a revelation.

Kade glanced over his shoulder toward the office door. He wanted this same feeling with Pippa. No, not the same feeling. He wanted something more, something profound. He wanted a soul-deep connection to the woman who carried his child. And not just because of that. He wanted to love her because she was Pippa.

Cash returned with a lidded cup and several packets

of sweetener. "I don't remember if she likes her tea hot either, but I do know she likes it sweet."

Kade's hand shook slightly as he reached for the cup. He stopped midgesture. Fisting and unfisting both hands, he took a moment to look at each one of his brothers. Doing so settled something in his chest, and his hand was now steady. "Thank you. All of you. For… everything."

Kade hoped they could hear and understand what he was really saying. Cord's hand tightened more. Chance and Cash both offered quick tucks of their chins and expressions that before this moment he would have found not only inscrutable but suspicious. Yeah, they understood, and wasn't that something?

Cash opened the door to his office but didn't look inside. He simply held it, and as Kade slipped through, he murmured, "We're here if and when you need us, bro. Chase and Clay will be on a plane in a heartbeat. All you have to do is ask."

The door snicked to a close behind him. Kade approached the couch warily. He held out the cup. "I thought maybe some hot tea…?"

Pippa's smile wavered a little and her eyes were moist but she accepted the cup and the sweetener packets. While she fixed the tea to her tastes, Kade located the afghan behind the pillows. It was soft and fluffy, and smelled faintly of dog. Roxanne wasn't the only one to use the blanket. Her dog Harley obviously liked it too. He shook it out and placed it over the back of the couch.

"You're taking care of me again."

He lifted a shoulder in a defensive movement then

forced himself to relax. "Yeah, I guess I am. Do you mind?"

She didn't quite meet his eyes. "Feels rather nice at the moment. Thank you."

"You're welcome."

Her gaze skittered to Cash's desk, the cup nestled in her hand forgotten. "Okay. Let's get this over with."

As he crossed the large office, Kade couldn't help but glance at the door. His brothers stood just on the other side. He almost stumbled as that weird sense of acceptance washed over him again. Why had he been fighting them all this time? He needed to do his own soul searching once Pippa's crisis was resolved. But today and the months to come were about her. His issues could wait.

Kade snagged the papers and all but marched back to the couch. He handed them to her and then, without asking, settled next to her and draped an arm around her shoulders. She leaned into him with a little sigh. She held up the first page and started reading.

Unlike when he'd scanned the report, Pippa read each line with deliberation. He watched her closely, squeezing her shoulders when she paled, backing slightly away when she jutted her chin with determination.

"She married two months after I was born," she whispered.

He didn't respond as she kept reading. Kade knew what was coming. Almost one year to the day after Pippa's birth, her sister Marcia Rae was born.

Pippa sucked in a breath and stiffened. Her hand shook so hard the papers she held rattled. When she finally spoke, she sounded broken. "It's like my mother just erased me. Like I never existed." Her eyes sought him, and he cupped her cheek in one hand, using his thumb to brush away the tears that had escaped. "How could she do that?"

Unable to stand it any longer, Kade retrieved the papers and set them on the coffee table. Then he scooped her up and settled her on his lap. She tucked her head against his shoulder and her tears flowed freely. Holding her, he rubbed his chin across the top of her head, dropping occasional kisses on her hair. And he waited until the storm of her hurt ebbed a little.

"I won't ever do that to my baby." Given the tears, her voice was remarkably strong as she made the vow.

"No, ladybug. You would never do that to our baby."

She pushed away so she could look at him. Her eyes still shimmered with unshed tears so he shifted slightly in order to reach his back pocket. He pulled out his bandanna and handed it to her. She wiped her eyes and dabbed at her nose but continued to look at him. She finally said, "I'm sorry, Kade."

Confused, he considered what she could possibly be apologizing for. Unable to figure it out, he asked, "What for?"

"For what I said about names not meaning anything. I was wrong." A little laugh that held a hint of hysteria escaped her. "*So* wrong. You were right. Names do have power. I mean, look at me. I didn't even know what my birth name was until two months ago. But after thinking about it, I knew it was *my* name. For some brief period of time, I was Marcia Rae Gore. I didn't know who that person was, or who she might have been, but I was settling into the idea that she was me at one time."

She paused to blow her nose and made an I'm-sorry-for-being-gross face at him. "And now, I discover there's another me. Who isn't me. She's my sister. It's like I never existed, even for that brief moment between birth and being named and my adoption when I became Pippa."

A tear tipped over her lashes and she brushed at it with the back of her hand. "Anyway, I understand now why you were so upset when you found out that you were a Barron. And I'm sorry for getting mad at you for doing the name change. I had no right."

Kade hugged her gently. "Shh, sweetheart. It's okay."

"No it's not."

He worked to stop the grin tugging at his mouth. "Are we going to fight over that now?"

She shook her head vehemently. "No. It was a stupid thing to fight over. I'd blame it on hormones, but I don't want to be a Pregzilla."

The tight knot in his chest that had started to loosen with his realization about his brothers all but unraveled. He really cared about Pippa and he wanted the chance to make a life with her, to become a real family.

"You? Hormonal?" He smiled and dropped a kiss on her forehead. "Never."

The next thing he knew, she was plastered to his chest, her arms around his neck. "Will you help me, Kade?"

He rubbed her back, gratified that her voice hadn't

caught and no sobs shook her body. "Of course I will. Whatever you need. Always."

She pushed back a second time, her expression determined. "I want to see her. Them. I want to see my mother and my sister."

Nineteen

Pippa stared at Kade's profile. Even before she'd walked away, she hadn't told him about her search. Instead of getting angry because she'd shut him out, he'd promised to help. And here he was, strong and sure, and ready to be her…her…whatever she needed him to be. And she definitely needed him, as they drove east toward the town where her mother lived.

She wasn't mad at him any longer. That feeling had quickly faded, overwhelmed by all the other emotions swamping her. At this point, she was no longer sure what she felt—except mostly numb. She'd been in a fog almost a month. Learning her sister, born barely a year after her, had the same name had hurt on a level she never before had experienced. It was as if she'd never existed. Or she'd been thrown away because she was defective. It left her broken with sharp slivers of pain slicing into her heart every time she thought about it.

And Kade had been there. He'd held her in his arms as she wept, even when she didn't know why the hot tears wouldn't stop. He didn't complain. And he'd stopped asking her to marry him. She wasn't sure how she felt about that now. He still hadn't given her the words. Not that she had any reason to complain. She hadn't offered an *I love you* to him either.

Turning away, she watched the mile markers zip past on I-40. Among all the shocks she'd received, the fact her birth family had been in Shawnee the whole time she was growing up was the one she focused on. Forty miles away. Her mother and siblings had been no farther than an hour's drive.

The past month had chafed at her. Cash and Chance had both ganged up on her and counseled caution. She hadn't listened until Carrie weighed in with the advice that Pippa would always wonder if she didn't meet the woman, that the not knowing would eat at her. Her best friend had never steered her wrong.

She'd waited another two weeks before asking Kade to accompany her. Pippa had considered driving herself but she was really showing now and got tired easily. Dr. Long kept telling her it was nothing to worry about but fear always crouched in the back of her mind. Warmth enveloped her hand and she looked down. Kade had wrapped his fingers around hers, his work-roughened skin familiar and soothing. Overloaded hormones or not, she was in love with Kade. He'd stepped up to be the responsible one. He'd been patient. And his actions showed how he felt. He might not have words to give her, but she'd bet there was love in his heart.

"Ask me again," she said. She snapped her mouth shut. What in the world was she thinking? Wasn't she glad he'd stopped badgering her about marriage? She wasn't ready for that step.

Kade ignored her while he flicked on the turn signal and changed lanes for the Shawnee exit. Maybe he hadn't heard. Maybe he didn't understand. Maybe he didn't want to embarrass her by saying he'd changed his mind. They could co-parent without being married. Hadn't she advocated for that very thing? Hadn't she demanded he admit out loud that he loved her? She no longer knew. Just as well he hadn't responded.

Following the directions from the navigation system, Kade drove them toward their destination. He squeezed her hand. "Breathe, ladybug. You got this."

Pippa shook her head. "No. I don't. What am I doing, Kade? How can I walk up to her and introduce myself? What do I say? Hello, I'm the other Marcia Rae. The one you gave away. The one you didn't love enough to keep."

Tears flowed as Kade suddenly veered into a parking lot. He was out of the truck and around to the passenger door in a flash. A moment later, she was in his arms. He smoothed a hand down her back, kissed her temple, made soothing noises.

"Shh, baby. We'll get through this. I'm here. Always. Never gonna leave you."

She knew then. Knew that if he did ask her to marry him again, she would say yes.

* * *

Kade should have released Pippa's hand so he could drive with both hands but he didn't. Tension rolled off her in waves and he worried. It couldn't be good for the baby and there was always the chance of her intense emotions triggering a migraine. She'd been so careful with medications during the pregnancy.

He turned onto the street where Pip's birth mother lived and slowly drove toward the address. There were cars parked there and people stood in the front yard. He pulled to the curb where they could watch but not be noticed. Pippa's face drained of color.

"Pip?"

"That…is that woman my mother? She doesn't look anything like me. Neither do those other people. This must be the wrong address."

A teenage boy and girl, probably fourteen and sixteen respectively, looked bored. Another boy and girl appeared to be college age, the girl maybe a bit older. They all had brown hair, as did the woman. The truck wasn't parked close enough that they could discern eye color or the finer nuances of the family's features. A man came out of the house and Pippa gasped. His blond hair, worn long and shaggy, was the exact shade of hers and there was a familiarity to the shape of his face. Kade had no doubt that Pippa's mother had married her birth father and had more children with him. The thought they'd thrown Pippa away burned in his gut.

"Let's go." Pippa's voice was so quiet and small he almost didn't hear her. "This isn't my family."

Turning toward her, worried that she was in denial,

Kade was surprised by the fierce determination on her face. He put the truck in Reverse and backed into an empty driveway. Pippa's mother looked up, stared, and he knew the moment the woman recognized her daughter. She extended her hand, took several steps toward the truck, and then Kade pulled into the street and drove away.

Pippa remained silent as they headed west on I-40, leaving Shawnee behind. Kade watched her as much as he could and still pay attention to traffic. Her color hadn't returned and he recognized the signs of pain pinching her features. He glanced down, realized her hands were pressed against her rounded abdomen.

"Ladybug?" He had to work to keep his voice calm.

"Something's not right," she whispered.

Kade—calm, cool, collected Kade—panicked. He was hitting ninety miles per hour when he hit Midwest City on the east side of the metro area. He didn't slow down when an Oklahoma state trooper pulled in behind him with lights and sirens. He dialed *55, connected to the highway patrol dispatch and explained the situation. The trooper pulled around him and led the way to University Hospital's Trauma One. Kade also alerted Savannah. He had her on speed dial.

He stopped at the ER doors and they were met by a gurney and nurses. He made it around to the passenger side just as someone grabbed his arm. He shook off the grip even as his brain registered who had touched him and what she was saying. Jolie. Cord's wife and an ER nurse.

"Breathe, Kade. We've got her." She glanced toward

the approaching trooper. "You deal with her then come inside. I'll get the information we need." She squeezed his arm and followed the gurney.

"That was some fancy driving there, slick."

He didn't have time for this. "Just write me the ticket, Trooper—" He glanced at the nameplate on the woman's uniform. "—Kincaid. I need to get inside."

"How far along is she?" The trooper's voice softened and she sounded sincerely concerned.

"Not far enough." His voice echoed the bleakness in his soul.

"Normally, I would lecture you that the smart thing would have been to stop and call an ambulance but while you were driving fast, you were in complete control. No ticket. Get in there with your wife."

The trooper's assumption made his chest hurt. Pippa wasn't his wife. Not yet. But she would be. "Thanks, ma'am."

She smiled. "Quincy. Quincy Kincaid. Ma'am makes me feel old."

Twenty minutes later, the ER was full of Barrons. Clay and Georgie were the only ones missing. They were back in Washington but Clay had called and told Kade they'd come if he asked. Overwhelmed, he didn't resist when Savvie took his phone. His attention was glued to the swinging doors separating the waiting area from the ER exam rooms. Savvie sat next to him, their shoulders brushing. The rest of the clan stood or sat in groups around the room.

When the doctor arrived, everyone surged to their

feet but only Savvie walked with Kade to meet Dr. Long and Jolie. Savvie squeezed his hand as the doctor spoke.

"Mom is going to be fine. The baby decided to wait a while longer to make an appearance." Dr. Long looked him up and down. "You're the father."

"Yes." He didn't apologize for growling the word.

"I want to keep her overnight just to be safe. She'll need lots of bed rest between now and January. My office will send you a list of do's and don'ts. C'mon back."

When he followed the doctor into the trauma room, the first thing he noticed was how pale and scared Pippa looked lying against the sheet covering the exam table. He wanted to scoop her into his arms, hug her, kiss her. He settled for sitting next to her and holding her hand. She squeezed his.

"We're gonna be okay. The baby and me."

"I know."

"I didn't mean to scare you."

Kade breathed out, made sure his hand remained gentle while wrapped around hers. "I can't lose you, Pippa. Can't lose our baby. Do you understand that?" She stared up at him but didn't reply. "Marry me. Marry me as soon as we can arrange it. If you hadn't asked for me, I wouldn't be here. I have no rights, not unless I'm your husband. Please, Pippa—" His voice broke. "Please marry me. I love you."

"Yes."

He looked up, unaware that he'd dropped his head until she spoke. "What did you say?" Had he really heard correctly?

She smiled. "Yes. I'll marry you."

Nurses arrived to get her ready for transfer to a private room and they shooed him out, but not before he kissed her.

When he walked back into the waiting area, he was immediately mobbed. He explained the doctor's orders and then Savvie hugged him tightly before facing the others. "I can tell by that big goofy grin he's wearing Pippa finally said yes."

He was overwhelmed by congratulations, hugs, thumps on his back, and it seemed that everyone was talking at once. Carrie had arrived while he was with Pippa and she whistled sharply. The noise level dropped immediately.

"All right then," Carrie commanded. "Ladies, we have a wedding to plan."

Kade started to object but Carrie cut him off. "I've been her BFF since we were five. I know exactly what kind of wedding she wants. And we're having it at the Crown B." She glowered at everyone. "Any problems with that?" No one dared disagree.

If he'd had his way, they would have been married at the courthouse on the way home from the hospital. His sisters-in-law and Carrie called him blasphemous. Today, as he stood in the backyard of the big house at the Crown B, he was glad the women had overruled him. A glowing and very pregnant Pippa approached him on Big John's arm. Family and friends surrounded them on this perfect November day. Pippa's eyes reflected the brilliant blue sky and her golden hair fell in loose waves around her face. Her gown was simple and appealed to Kade on an elemental level.

His mother, Rose, stood with Miz Beth. Both women were beaming. He wished his grandparents could have been there. William and Ramona had played a big role in his life. Bill was gone and advance Alzheimer's kept Ramona hospitalized.

The scare over the baby had Pippa cracking open a door for her parents. She'd relented and they were here for the marriage ceremony, though Pippa didn't want David Duncan to walk her down the aisle. She hadn't forgiven them that much yet.

Big John placed Pippa's hand in Kade's and they turned to face Judge Nelligan. Words were said, vows given and accepted. When the judge called for the rings, Kade turned to Clay. He didn't have a best man—he had five. CJ, Cord's son, and now Kade's nephew, acted as ring bearer. The boy handed the ring to Cash, who stood at the end of the line. The ring passed from brother to brother in birth order until Clay handed it to Kade.

Pippa didn't have all that fanfare. Carrie merely took the ring off her thumb and placed it on Pippa's palm. Once the rings were exchanged, the judge pronounced them husband and wife. They kissed to a round of cheers and Kade swept Pippa up in his arms to carry her into the house. He intended for her to sit for the duration of their reception. CJ escorted Carrie, much to the kid's embarrassment, and each of Kade's brothers fell in behind with their wives.

Life was good. He and Pippa would have Thanksgiving, Christmas and the New Year, then they would welcome their baby into the world. Life couldn't get much better than this. Kade had everything he'd ever wanted—and a lot he'd never dared hope for.

"Hello, Mrs. Barron."

"Hi there, Mr. Barron."

And that name didn't sound so unfamiliar after all.

Epilogue

Kade didn't panic. He'd carefully timed Pippa's contractions. They had plenty of time to get to the birthing center in Oklahoma City. The snow from the storm the previous week had melted. The roads were clear. Once the truck hit the interstate, he kept the speed at a steady five miles over the speed limit. As promised, he'd started what Cassie called the Family Phone Tree, a phrase she always placed in air quotes.

"Babies never come at convenient times," Pippa groused.

"Where's the fun in that? Savvie was gloating about waking everyone." He squeezed her hand. "You doing okay?"

She nodded, winced, caught her breath and squeezed his hand. Hard. He nudged the speed up a little. "Almost there, ladybug. And since it's three in the morning, no traffic. That's good."

When he pulled up at the birthing center, the whole group was already gathered. Cash grabbed his keys. Cord grabbed Pippa's bag. Within minutes, Pippa was checked in and settled in a suite. Dr. Long arrived shortly after and while she was examining Pippa, Kade stepped out. He was met in the waiting room by a group of smiling faces and Savvie holding out a cup of hot black coffee.

"Don't even try to tell us to go home. Not happenin', big bro. And I've called your mom. Rose is on her way."

The lump in his throat almost choked him as he looked around at his brothers, his sisters. And he knew. He truly was a Barron. And that was a good thing.

Kade stared at the red-faced baby in Pippa's arms. After eight hours of labor, the birth had been relatively easy. *Relatively* being the operative word. His heart was ready to burst out of his chest. "I am so proud of you, sweetheart."

Pippa beamed at him then gazed at their daughter. "We did good, didn't we?"

"No ladybug, *you* did. I just stood here and got in the way."

She laughed and he breathed easier. Watching their daughter come into the world had been life changing. He'd helped birth foals and calves and always marveled at the miracle of birth and life, but until he cut the umbilical cord on their baby? He'd had no idea how profoundly it would affect him. Nor did he know how deep his capacity to love would become. He loved Pippa and their baby with his whole heart. No, he loved them with his entire being. He claimed both of them then and there. Forever.

One of the nurses appeared on the other side of the bed. "She has a ten Apgar score, which is perfect. What are you going to name her?"

Pippa gazed up at him. "I want to name her Ruth, for my grandmother."

"Whatever you want, ladybug." Kade barely got the words out.

"And Ramona for yours."

Moisture in his eyes blinded him as he slipped his arm beneath her, cradling his wife and their child. "She's beautiful. And perfect, our Ruth Ramona," he murmured against Pippa's temple. "Just like her mother."

Then the horde came, wanting to see baby Ruth, to congratulate. Brothers and sisters-in-law. Cousins. Even Pippa's parents, who were clutching a fuzzy teddy bear and flowers. Clay eventually drew Kade out into the hallway where all his brothers had gathered.

"We need to talk, Kade." Clay looked somber.

"What's wrong?"

"Nothing," Cord answered. "We just want you to know that the ranch truly is yours."

"And that includes the big house," Chance added.

Chase grinned at him. "We want someone living there who loves it like we did. Who will make the big house a home again."

"It's built for kids and family gatherings. Which means you're stuck with Thanksgiving and Christmas from now on," Cash chimed in.

Kade eventually got a word in edgewise. "What about Big John and Miz Beth? They—"

Chase cut him off. "Whose idea do you think this is? They want something small and cozy."

"But where will they go?"

Cord thumped him on the back. "They've already gone. About a quarter of a mile away. We moved your stuff into the big house and their belongings into the manager's. Even trade."

"We're family, Kade. You. Pippa. Baby Ruth. All of us," the brothers said in unison.

Kade was a simple man and he'd discovered what was important. His wife. His baby girl. His brothers. Family. He'd found and claimed his in the most unlikely of places. And he was a happy man because of it.

* * * * *

*Don't miss any of these cowgirl romances from
Silver James*

*COWGIRLS DON'T CRY
THE COWGIRL'S LITTLE SECRET
THE BOSS AND HIS COWGIRL
CONVENIENT COWGIRL BRIDE
REDEEMED BY THE COWGIRL*

Available now from Harlequin Desire!

***

*If you're on Twitter, tell us what you think
of Harlequin Desire! #harlequindesire*

Read on for a sneak peek of
DOWN HOME COWBOY
by New York Times *bestselling author*
Maisey Yates.
When rancher and single dad Cain Donnelly moves
to Copper Ridge, Oregon, to make a fresh start with
his teenage daughter, the last thing he wants is to risk
his heart again. So why can't he keep his eyes—or
his hands—off Alison Davis, the one woman in town
guaranteed to complicate his life?

"Hey, Bo," Cain called, looking around the kitchen and living room area for his daughter, who was on the verge of being late for her second week on the job. "Are you ready to go?"

He heard footsteps hit the bottom landing, followed by a disgusted noise. "Do you have to call me that?"

"Yes," he said, keeping his tone serious. "Though I could always go back to the full name. Violet Beauregarde the Walking Blueberry." She'd thought that nod to *Charlie and the Chocolate Factory* was great. Back when she was four and all he'd had to do was smile funny to get her to belly laugh.

"Pass."

"I have to call you at least one horrifying nickname a week. All the better if it slips out in public."

"Is there public in Copper Ridge? Because I've yet to see it."

"Hey, you serve the public as part of your job at the bakery."

"The presence of humanity does not mean the presence of culture."

"Chill out, Sylvia Plath. Your commitment to being angry at the world is getting old." He shook his head, looking at his dark-haired, green-eyed daughter, who was now edging closer to being a woman than being that round, rosy-cheeked little girl he still saw in his mind's eye.

"Well, you don't have to bear witness to it today. Lane is giving me a ride into town."

Cain frowned. He still hadn't been in to see Violet at work. In part because she clearly didn't want him to. But he had assumed that once she was established and feeling independent she wouldn't mind if he took her to Pie in the Sky.

Apparently, she did.

"Great," he said. "I have more work to do around here anyway."

"The life of a dairy farmer is never dull. Well, no, it's always dull. It just never stops." Violet walked over to the couch where she had deposited her purse yesterday and picked it up. "Same with baking pies, I guess."

"Are you ready to go, Violet?" Lane came breezing into the room looking slightly disheveled, Cain's younger brother Finn closely behind her, also looking suspiciously mussed.

Absolutely no points for guessing what they had just been up to. Though he could see that Violet was oblivious. If she had guessed, she wouldn't be able to hide her reaction. Which warmed his heart in a way. That his teenage daughter was still pretty innocent about some things. That she was still young in some ways.

Hard to retain any sort of innocence when your mother abandoned you. And since he knew all about parental abandonment and how much it screwed with you, he was even angrier that his daughter was going through the same thing.

"Ready," Violet responded.

Even though it was a one-word answer, it lacked the edge usually involved in her responses to him. He supposed being jealous of his brother's girlfriend was a little bit ridiculous.

"Have fun," he said, just because he knew it would irritate her.

He had lost the power to make her laugh. To make her smile, with any kind of ease. So, he supposed he would just embrace his ability to irritate.

At least he excelled at that.

He could tell he had excelled yet again when she didn't smile at him as she left the room with Lane.

"Wait," Finn said, walking past him and grabbing Lane around the waist, turning her and kissing her deep.

It was all Cain could do to keep from groaning audibly. Between his horndog younger brothers and his incredibly happy other brother, he felt like sex was being thrown in his face constantly. Except not in a fun way that involved him having it.

Lane and Violet left, and Finn walked back into the living room. "I'm going to marry that woman," he said, the self-satisfied grin on his face scraping at Cain's current irritation.

"Have you asked her yet?"

"Not officially. But I'm going to. I want to spend the rest of my life with her."

"That's a long time. Trust me. Married years are different than regular years." He had way too much experience living with somebody who didn't even like him anymore. Way too much experience walking quietly through his own house so that he could avoid the conversation that needed to be had, or avoid the silence that seemed magnified when the two of them were in the same room.

He didn't think Finn would suffer the same fate, though. Finn and Lane had known each other for years, and they had been friends before they were a couple. Cain and Kathleen had been stupid and young. He had gotten her pregnant and wanted to do the right thing, instead of doing the kind of thing his father would do.

All in all, it wasn't the best foundation for a marriage.

For a while, they had tried. Both of them. He wasn't really sure when they had stopped.

"I hope you're right," Finn said, obnoxiously cheerful. "I hope every year with Lane feels like five. Because my time with her has been the best of my life."

Given the way they had grown up, Cain really didn't begrudge Finn his happiness. He was glad for his brother, in a way. When he wasn't busy feeling irritated by his own celibate status.

Though, in fairness to him, figuring out how to conduct a physical relationship while he was raising a teenage girl was pretty tricky. He had to set some kind of example. And casual sex wasn't exactly the one he was aiming for.

"Good for you," he said, sounding more annoyed than he had intended.

"How's the barn coming along?"

Cain was grateful for the change in subject. "It's coming."

"Show me."

His brother grabbed his hat off the shelf by the door, and Cain grabbed his own. Strange how this had become somewhat natural. How sharing a space with Finn, Alex and Liam—while annoying on occasion—was just starting to be life.

He took the steps on the front porch two at a time, inhaling the sharp, clear air. It was late summer, and in Texas about now walking outside would be like getting wrapped in a wet blanket. That was also on fire. He could honestly say he didn't miss that part of his adopted home state.

The Oregon coast ran a little cold for his taste, but he had to admit it was still nicer than sweltering. The wind whipped up, filtering through the pine trees and kicking up the smell of wood, hay and horse. If green had a smell, it would be that smell that rode the coastal air across the mountains. Fresh and heavy, all at the same time.

It was fastest to take a truck out to the old barn on the property, the one that had originally stood near the first house that had been built when their great-grandparents had bought the land. The house was long gone, but the barn still remained, and with all of his near-nonexistent free time, Cain had been fashioning the place into a house for Violet and himself.

After they parked, he and his brother walked through the still overgrown pathway that led up to the old barn.

"Wow," Finn said, stepping deeper into the room. "You've done a lot."

"New wiring," Cain said, gesturing broadly. "Insulation, Sheetrock. I need to work on interior walls. But, yeah, it's coming along. It will be fine for the two of us for the next couple of years. And when Violet leaves..."

Unbidden, an image of the beautiful redhead he had seen across the bar last night filtered into his mind's eye. Yeah, in a couple of years he would have a place to bring a woman like that.

Not that he couldn't go back to her place, or get a hotel, but he didn't want to have to explain his absence to a teenage girl who barely thought of him as human, much less wanted to realize he was actually just a guy with a sex drive and everything. Both of them would probably die from the humiliation of that.

"It'll be a pretty nice place," Finn said, and Cain was grateful his younger brother couldn't read his mind.

"Not bad. I know that I could pay somebody to finish it. But right now I'm kind of enjoying the therapy. I spent a long time managing things. Managing a big ranch, not actually working it. Managing my marriage instead of actually working at it. I'm ready to be hands-on again. This is the life that I'm choosing to build for myself. So I guess I better build it."

He knew that at thirty-eight his feelings of midlife angst were totally unearned, but having his wife leave had forced him into kind of a strange crisis point. One where he had started asking himself if that was it. If everything good that he was going to do was behind him.

So, he had left the ranch in Texas—the one he had

spent so many years building up—walked away with a decent chunk of change, and packed his entire life up, packed his kid up, and gone to the West Coast to find… Something else to do. Something else to be. To find a way to reconnect with Violet.

So far, he'd found ranch work and little else. Violet still barely tolerated him in spite of everything he was doing to try to fix their lives, and he didn't feel any closer to moving forward than he had back in Texas.

He was just moved.

Finn's phone buzzed and he pulled it out of his pocket to check his texts. "Hey," he said, "can you pick up Violet tonight from work?"

"I thought Lane was doing it."

"It's her girls' night thing. She forgot."

Well, he had just been thinking that he needed to actually see where Violet worked. "Sure. Sounds good."

"What are you going to do until then?"

"I figured I would do some work in here."

Finn pushed his sleeves up, smiling. "Mind if I help?"

"Sure," Cain said. "Grab a hammer."

ALISON STARED AT the sunken cake sitting on the kitchen countertop and frowned. Then quickly erased the frown so that Violet wouldn't see it.

"I don't know what happened," Violet said, looking perturbed.

"You probably took it out too early. It's nothing a little extra icing can't fix. And it's my girls' night tonight, so I think it can be of use in that environment rather than being put up for sale."

Violet screwed up her face. "It's ugly."

"An ugly cake is still cake. As long as it doesn't have raisins it's fine."

"Oh, I didn't put any raisins in it."

Alison was slightly amused that her newest employee seemed to know about her raisin aversion, even if she didn't quite have cooking times down. Violet was a good employee, but she had absolutely no experience baking. For the most part, Alison had put her on the register, which she had picked up much faster than kitchen duties. But she tried to set aside a certain amount of time every shift to give Violet a chance to get some experience with the actual baking part of the bakery.

Maybe it wasn't as necessary to do with a teenager who had her first job as it was to do with some of the other women who came through the shop, desperately in need of work experience after years out of the workforce, but Alison was applying the same principles to Violet as she did to everyone else.

Right now she was short on staff, and even shorter on people who had the skill level she required with the baked goods to do any training. So while she could farm out Violet's register training, the cakes, pies and other pastries had to be done by her.

"I'll do better next time," Violet said, sounding determined. Which encouraged Alison, because Violet hadn't sounded anything like determined when she had first come in looking for work. Violet was a sullen teenager of the first order. And even though she most definitely made an attempt to put on a good show for

Alison, she was clearly in a full internal battle with her feelings on authority figures.

Having been a horrific teenager herself, Alison felt some level of sympathy for her. But also very little patience. Fortunately, Violet seemed to react well to her brand of no-nonsense response to attitude.

"You will do better next time," Alison said, "because I can eat one mistake cake, but if I have to continue eating them, my jeans aren't going to fit and then I'm going to have to buy new jeans, and that's going to have to come out of your paycheck."

She patted Violet on the shoulder then walked through the double doors that led from the kitchen and behind the counter. The shop was in its late-afternoon lull. A little too close to dinner for most people to be stopping in for pieces of pie.

A rush of air blew into the shop and Alison looked up just in time to see a tall, muscular man walk in through the blue door. A pang of recognition hit her in the chest before she even got a good look at him. She didn't need a good look at him. Because just like the first time she'd seen him, on the other side of Ace's bar, the feeling he created inside of her wasn't logical, wasn't cerebral. It was physical. It lived in her, and it superseded control.

For somebody who prized control, it was an affront on multiple levels.

He lifted his head and confirmed what her jittering nerves already knew. That beneath that dark cowboy hat was the face of the man who had most definitely been looking at her at the bar the night before.

He hadn't left town. He hadn't been a hallucinogenic expression of a fevered imagination. And he had found her.

The twist of attraction turned into something else, just for a moment. A strange kind of panic that she hadn't confronted for a long time. That somehow this man had found out who she was, had tracked her down.

No. That's not it. Even if he did, that doesn't make him crazy. It doesn't.

And more than likely he was just here for a piece of pie. She took a deep breath, steeling herself to look directly at him. Which was... Wow. He was hotter than she remembered. And that was saying something. She had first spotted him in the dim light of the bar, with a healthy amount of space between them.

Now, well, now the daylight was bright, and he was very close. And he was magnificent. The way that black T-shirt hugged all those muscles bordered on obscene, his dark green eyes like the deep of the forest beckoning her to draw close. Except, unlike the forest, his eyes didn't promise solitude and inner peace. No, it was something much more carnal. Or maybe that was just her aforementioned overheated imagination.

His jaw was covered by a neatly trimmed dark beard, and she would normally have said she wasn't a huge fan, but something about the beard on him was like flaunting an excess of testosterone. And she was in a very testosterone-starved state. So it was like stumbling onto water in a desert.

Of course, all of that hyperbole was simply that. His eyes weren't actually promising her anything; in fact, his expression was blank. And she realized that while he might look sexier to her today than he had that night, she might look unrecognizable to him.

Last night she had been wearing an outfit that at least hinted at the fact that she had a female figure. And she'd had makeup on. Plus, she'd gone to the effort to straighten her mass of auburn hair. Today, it was its glorious frizzy self, piled on top of her head, half captured in a rubber band, half pinned down with a pen. And as for makeup… Well, on days when she had to be at the bakery early, that was just not a happening thing.

Her apron disguised her figure, and beneath it, the button-up striped shirt that she had tucked into her jeans wasn't exactly vixen wear.

"Can I…? Can I help you?" She tucked a stray strand of hair behind her ear and found herself tilting her head to the side, her body apparently calling on all of the flirtation skills it hadn't used since she was eighteen years old.

Very immature, underdeveloped skills.

Suddenly, her lips felt dry, so she had to lick them. And when she did, heat flared in those forest green eyes that made her think maybe he did recognize her. Or, if he didn't, maybe his body did. Just like hers recognized his. *Oh, Lord.*

"Yes," he said, his voice much more…taciturn than she had imagined it might be. She hadn't realized until that moment that she had built something of a narrative around him. Brooding, certainly, because he had most definitely been brooding in the bar, but she had imagined he might flirt with a lazy drawl. Of course, it was difficult to tell with one word, but his voice had been clipped. Definitely clipped.

"I have a lot of different pie. I mean, a lot of different kinds. So, if you need suggestions…or a list… I can help."

"I'm not here for pie. I'm here to pick up my daughter…"

Pick up DOWN HOME COWBOY,
the latest COPPER RIDGE novel
from Maisey Yates and HQN Books!

#2533 THE CEO'S NANNY AFFAIR

Billionaires and Babies • by Joss Wood

When billionaire Linc Ballantyne's ex abandons not one, but *two* children, he strikes up a wary deal with her too-sexy sister. She'll be the nanny and they'll keep their hands to themselves. But their temporary truce soon becomes a temporary tryst!

#2534 TEMPTED BY THE WRONG TWIN

Texas Cattleman's Club: Blackmail • by Rachel Bailey

Harper Lake is pregnant, but the father isn't who she thinks—it's her boss's identical twin brother! Wealthy former Navy SEAL Nick Tate pretended to be his brother as a favor, and now he's proposing a marriage of convenience that just might lead to real romance...

#2535 THE TEXAN'S BABY PROPOSAL

Callahan's Clan • by Sara Orwig

Millionaire Texan Marc Medina must marry immediately to inherit his grandfather's ranch. When his newly single secretary tells him she's pregnant, he knows a brilliant deal when he sees one. He'll make her his wife...and have her in his bed!

#2536 LITTLE SECRETS: CLAIMING HIS PREGNANT BRIDE by Sarah M. Anderson

Restless—that's businessman and biker Seth Bolton. But when he rescues pregnant runaway bride Kate Burroughs, he wants much more than he should with the lush mom-to-be... But she won't settle for anything less than taming his heart!

#2537 FROM TEMPTATION TO TWINS

Whiskey Bay Brides • by Barbara Dunlop

When Juliet Parker goes home to reopen her grandfather's restaurant, she clashes with her childhood crush, tycoon Caleb Watford, who's building a rival restaurant. Then the stakes skyrocket after their one night leaves her expecting two little surprises!

#2538 THE TYCOON'S FIANCÉE DEAL

The Wild Caruthers Bachelors • by Katherine Garbera

Derek Caruthers promised his best friend that their fake engagement would end after he'd secured his promotion...but what's a man of honor to do when their red-hot kisses prove she's the only one for him?

YOU CAN FIND MORE INFORMATION ON UPCOMING HARLEQUIN® TITLES, FREE EXCERPTS AND MORE AT WWW.HARLEQUIN.COM.

HDCNM0717

Get 2 Free Books,
Plus 2 Free Gifts—
just for trying the Reader Service!

*When billionaire Linc Ballantyne's ex abandons not
one, but two children, he strikes up a wary deal with her
too-sexy sister. She'll be the nanny and they'll keep their
hands to themselves. But their temporary truce soon
becomes a temporary tryst!*

Read on for a sneak peek at
THE CEO'S NANNY AFFAIR
by Joss Wood.

Why Linc had ever agreed to meet with his ex-fiancée's
sister was confounding. But he'd heard something in her
voice, a note of panic and sorrow. Maybe something had
happened to Kari, and, if so, he needed to know what.
She was still his son's mother, after all.

Linc heard the light rap on the door and sucked in a
breath.

His first thought when he opened his front door to Tate
Harper was that he wanted her. Under him, on top of him,
up against the nearest wall…any way he could have her.

That thought was immediately followed by *Oh, crap,
not again.*

He knew the Harpers were trouble. Kari had been a
stunning woman, but her beauty, as he knew—and paid
for—had taken work. The woman standing behind the
stroller was effortlessly gorgeous. Her hair was a riot of

blond and brown, eyes the color of his favorite whiskey under arched eyebrows, and her skin, makeup-free, was flawless. This Harper sister's beauty was all natural and, dammit, so much more potent.

Linc, his hand on the doorknob, took a moment to draw in some much-needed air.

"Tate? Come on in."

She pushed the stroller into the hall with a white-knuckled grip. Linc, wincing at the realization that he was allowing a whole bunch of trouble to walk through his front door, was about to rescind his invitation. Then he made the mistake of looking into her eyes.

She'd jumped into the ring with Kari and had the crap kicked out of her, Linc realized. And, for some reason, she thought he could help her clean up the mess. And because his first instinct was to protect, to make things right, he wanted to wipe the fear from Tate's expression.

Linc closed his eyes and reminded himself to start using his brain.

He needed to hear Tate's story so he could hustle her out the door and get back to his predictable, safe, sensible world. She was pure temptation, and being attracted to his crazy ex's sister was a complication he most definitely did not need.

Don't miss
THE CEO'S NANNY AFFAIR
by Joss Wood, available August 2017 wherever
Harlequin® Desire books and ebooks are sold.

www.Harlequin.com

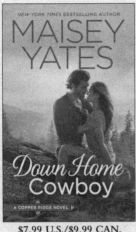

LOVE
Harlequin
romance?

Join our Harlequin community to share your thoughts and connect with other romance readers!

Be the first to find out about promotions, news, and exclusive content!

Sign up for the Harlequin e-newsletter and download a free book from any series at

www.TryHarlequin.com

CONNECT WITH US AT:

Harlequin.com/Community

 Facebook.com/HarlequinBooks

 Twitter.com/HarlequinBooks

 Instagram.com/HarlequinBooks

 Pinterest.com/HarlequinBooks

ReaderService.com

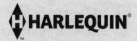

**ROMANCE WHEN
YOU NEED IT**

HSOCIAL2017

Want to give in to temptation with
steamy tales of irresistible desire?

Check out **Harlequin® Presents®**,
Harlequin® Desire and
Harlequin® Kimani™ Romance books!

New books available every month!

CONNECT WITH US AT:

Harlequin.com/Community

 Facebook.com/HarlequinBooks

 Twitter.com/HarlequinBooks

 Instagram.com/HarlequinBooks

 Pinterest.com/HarlequinBooks

ReaderService.com

**ROMANCE WHEN
YOU NEED IT**

PGENRE2017